The Oxford Street Coffee House Detectives and the Case of the Young Patrician Lady

Alydia Rackham

Published by Alydia Rackham, 2024.

THE OXFORD STREET COFFEE HOUSE DETECTIVES AND THE CASE OF THE YOUNG PATRICIAN LADY

First edition. April 16, 2024.

ISBN: 979-8224242337

Written by Alydia Rackham.

Chapter One: "The Painting Without a Master"

As told by
MISS ELSIE JONES
London
April 9th, 1890

MY NAME IS ELSIE JONES. My very few close friends call me by my first name, and Mr. McDougal calls me "Miss Jones." Everyone else in this noisy, smoky town—be he a statesman or a chimney sweep—addresses me as "Miss Else." That is the way it has been since I was born in a little flat above a store in Covent Garden, and I'll be known by that name until I am an old maid, I suppose.

Prudence would dictate that I restrain the subjects of this journal to the weather and the idle chat between acquaintances—or even the expected prattling of a girl in love. But unfortunately, as my colleagues will tell you, I do not muse about such silliness. The subjects that occupy my thoughts are infinitely more important—and secret, and dangerous. And as my colleagues will also tell you, I keep my important thoughts to myself. But I must process, and arrange, and study them somehow—which leaves me with the pages of this journal. I can only hope it does not fall into the wrong hands.

I decided to begin this journal to gather details and impressions after the events of today—events that may prove to be vital later on. I will thus begin with this morning, and include as much as I can remember.

I woke up to the sound of the chime on my clock mantle striking six. I lay there a moment, then sat up, my mattress squeaking. I sighed, pushed my hair out of my face, and slid out from underneath my heavy blankets to put my feet in my slippers. I always hate that first few moments after getting out from under warm blankets and step into the icy open air of my apartment. I arose, and took down my housecoat and, shivering, pulled it on, then lit a lamp. The small flame illuminated my little, low-ceilinged apartment and its neat, small furnishings.

I put on my clothes—a simple brown dress that fit my slender form, and black shoes—and brushed my long, black hair, then pinned it up. I wore one piece of jewelry, one that I always wore: it was my mother's necklace, with a gold chain and a sapphire stone, which brings out the unusual vibrancy of my blue of my eyes, contrasted with my pale skin. I have always known my eyes to be my only beauty, and thus I do not worry overmuch about my appearance.

After finishing my toilette, I put on my coat and scarf, and pinned on my straw hat, and put out my lamp. I took up my purse and left my small house, locking my door behind me. My long keys rattled on their ring. I ascended the steps, for I live in a basement apartment, and pushed open the thick door to greet the chilly, foggy morning.

London is eerie in the early dark. The gray fog crouches between the buildings, muffling all sound, disguising distant pedestrians as phantoms. Here and there, street lamps cast circles of dim light, like torches over a bog. The scent of baking bread and burning coal wafted as I passed several low windows. My flat-heeled shoes were silent on the dirty cobbles as I walked swiftly through the narrow alleys.

Wooden soles tapped behind me—quick steps, long strides. I did not bother to turn, and ducked my head to hide a smile as a young man caught up to walk beside me.

"Elsie, I have asked you to wait for me more than a dozen times," his low, almost musical tones scolded. I kept my attention ahead of me.

"I've walked this way a *thousand* times, Jack," I replied in a low voice. "Nothing dreadful has befallen me yet."

"It could," he answered. "It isn't safe for a lady to walk alone in the dark."

I could not bear to argue with him—I never could. I sneaked a glance at him as we passed beneath a crooked streetlamp. I can most simply describe John "Jack" Young as tall, dark and handsome. He always wears a long brown coat when out walking, and a short brown top hat. He has warm auburn eyes, a clean-shaven face and dark hair that he keeps well-combed, but he can never tame that one curl that usually falls across his forehead. I cast a sweeping look around us, checking the windows. I saw no one.

"Any news?" I asked Jack under my breath.

"Perhaps," he said, equally low. "An oil may have given someone the slip."

I looked at him in surprise.

"More later," he assured me, and his bright eyes twinkled when I scowled.

We rounded several twisting corners, and came at last to the low back door of a tall, brick building. I got in my purse and pulled out my jingling keys, then shoved one into the iron lock. The bolt clacked as it threw, and the door creaked as I opened it. We stepped inside, and I reached to my left to take up a box of matches from the counter and lit an oil lamp. Jack stepped inside behind me and shut the door. Shivering, I held my hands over the top of the lamp for a moment before bending to light the huge stove.

"It always seemed colder in here than outside," Jack muttered, moving to light two more lamps and banish the dark from the main back room. I slammed the iron door of the stove shut, put my hands on my hips and made a quick assessment of the wooden shelves and counters that filled this short room. There lay the huge burlap sacks bulging with raw coffee from Arabia and Africa, there huddled the buckets for carrying beans to the roaster—all in a row—there stood the barrels of already-roasted black beans, there hung the sinks and pumps for washing the dozens of plain mugs that now packed the tall shelves like books in a great library. On an opposite counter, the three great coffee pots stood like soldiers. Off to my left the tea was stored, and everything that went with it: cups, saucers, pots and trays, and the ice-box for the creamer and milk. In the center waited the stocky work table, clear except for the two large grinders bolted to its corners. Everything was spotless and orderly—exactly the way I had left it the night before.

Jack took off his hat and hung it on the peg near the door, then stamped his feet on the stone floor and puffed into his hands. A cloud of vapor issued. I smirked at him, but did not say anything, and took off my own hat.

Jack turned and scooped two small bucketfuls of black beans from the nearest barrel, and came back to the table. He handed one to me, and simultaneously, we dumped the beans into our respective grinders and began working the noisy cranks, sending grounds as black as gunpowder flowing out into the buckets on the other side.

"Tell me about the oil," I said over the noise, but Jack just smiled and kept his secret, while I fumed.

After filling the buckets with grounds, I turned to making scones while Jack flagged down the ice man outside. He came back in hauling a huge block of ice—I held the ice box open so he could set it inside. A few minutes later, Jack kept the scones from burning while I took the bottles of milk from the milkman and hefted them into the ice box. As you can imagine, my hands have grown tough from this kind of work. Then, Jack and I set about brewing large pots of coffee, which quickly warmed up the room.

"Which oil is it?" I pressed Jack as soon as I set the water to draining through the last maker. "Would I know it?"

"No, because *I* do not know it," Jack sighed. "It is merely a fairly accurate bit of rumor that I caught the hearing of while leaving the Oxford last night. I told Mr. McDougal straightaway and he should have the report from later this morning."

"What did you hear?" I demanded, watching his face closely. But he did not look at me—only chuckled, and pulled out his pocket watch.

"We have finished just in time—we are getting much quicker."

I bit my cheek at his change of subject, but knew he would not yield any more. I sighed, took off my coat and pulled my apron from its hook.

"Yes, well, it goes twice as fast with two people here."

"I know!" he cried, pulling down his own apron—a different one—that belonged to a clerk. "Once I realized that you were arriving here at half past *four* in the morning so you could complete it all in time to open, I had to do something about it."

I gave him a crooked smile as I tied my apron.

"Thank you, Jack. It makes my morning much more pleasant."

He flashed me a grin.

"Yes, having half the work load is quite a bit more pleasant, I would imagine."

That had not been quite what I had meant, but I of course did not elaborate. I pulled out my own little pocket watch, checked the time, looked at Jack and slipped into an effortless, broad cockney dialect.

"Well, Cap'n, it's time to open, I fink!"

He laughed, and I strode forward and heaved open the large door that led to the main room of the Oxford Street Coffee House.

This room had a tall wooden ceiling, a fireplace at each end, wooden floors and walls, a coffee bar nearer the back room, and a spiral staircase in the far corner that led to the second storey.

It was dark and cold in here, too, but John and I quickly lit leaping fires in each fireplace, and set flame to the many lamps. Soon, the wide room was filled with warm golden light and warmth, and I unbolted the main door with good conscience.

Instantly, five old men—Mr. Withersworth, Mr. Cambridge, Mr. Wilder, Mr. Arthur and Mr. Cogsmith bustled in, stamping their feet and pulling off their hats.

"Good heavens, Miss Else, you kept us waiting long enough!" Mr. Withersworth, a sallow-faced old gentleman, complained. "We almost caught our deaths waiting on the front steps."

"Blimey, it ain't even eight o'clock yet," I retorted. "If ye'd come any earlier, you'd 'ave to *chew* the grounds!"

They all muttered various comments of dissent, none of which I listened to, and I shut the door behind them. They hung up their coats and hats, then gathered around their usual circular table in the center of the room. I had often tried to get them to sit closer to the fire, but they refused. They were the type of gentlemen who enjoyed good-naturedly complaining about everything in general, and without an object of complaint, they were at a loss.

"I don't know what she's thinking of, keeping us waiting like that," Mr. Withersworth continued. "And even now, I cannot feel my feet for the cold!"

"You can never feel your feet, Henry," Mr. Cambridge answered. "I don't know when the last time was that you bought new boots—those are quite full of holes!"

"They are full of holes from all the confounded walking you gentlemen force me to do before coming here," he retorted. "And for what? You cannot persuade me that smog and filth are good for one's constitution!"

I smiled so they could not see as I slipped into the back room and snatched up a great coffee pot and a handful of mugs. I turned back around to see Jack poking his head through the door.

"Do you need help?"

I gave him a severe look.

"Go to your desk before they see you," I hissed. He only smiled, turned and headed back through the great room toward his office.

I returned to the gentlemen's table and set the coffee cups down before Mr. Withersworth, Mr. Cambridge, and Mr. Wilder, then poured the steaming coffee for them. I then darted back into the back room and fixed the tea and carried out the tray for Mr. Arthur and Mr. Cogsmith. As I was handing them their cups and saucers, I caught a snatch of a comment that made me linger.

"—quite the fantastic collection of paintings down at the Smith," Mr. Arthur, a rather fat mustached man, said. "Do any of you gentlemen know whose they are?"

The gentlemen muttered and bumbled, and Mr. Wilder, a long-bearded, bespectacled gentleman, looked down his nose, frowned, and said:

"I had heard it was Da Vinci—and perhaps some done by his apprentices."

I stopped where I was, holding the tray limp in my left hand, staring at him.

"Yes, I heard of it from one of the museum clerks last week," Mr. Withersworth added.

"But they have tried to keep the show's content a secret until the grand opening tomorrow night," Mr. Cogsmith puffed. "A very posh affair, that. Invitation only."

"Is it indeed!" the rest of them commented, and began asking each other if anyone he knew had been invited.

"Miss Else!" Mr. Arthur suddenly bellowed. I jumped.

"Yes?"

"You look as if we were speaking Latin, girl," he laughed. I raised my eyebrows.

"Did you say Da Vinci?"

"I believe Mr. Wilder said that, yes," Mr. Withersworth said. I waited. Then, all the gentlemen began chuckling and shaking their heads. I looked back at them placidly.

"She has no idea who he is, poor girl," Mr. Cambridge, a tall, pleasant-faced man smiled. "Come here, my dear, and we shall educate you!"

I kept my expression clear and moved over to stand beside him. He took brief, friendly hold of my elbow.

"So you've never learned who Da Vinci was, eh?"

"Aaoow, anything I learn is from you gentlemen," I lied, giving extra vulgarity to my dialect. They all chuckled, flattered.

"He was one of the great Renaissance painters," Mr. Cambridge explained. "Perhaps only equaled by Michelangelo. One of Da Vinci's most famous and mysterious paintings is the Mona Lisa—I wonder if it is traveling in this show?" He glanced at his friends. They shook their heads, indicating that they did not know. I tilted my head at Mr. Cambridge.

"And wat's this 'ere Mona Lisa a picture of?" I asked, then secretly enjoyed the uproar this caused, especially when Mr. Withersworth wondered if I had ever been outside this coffee house.

"Why, my dear, it's a portrait!" Mr. Cambridge said. "A portrait of a woman."

"Aaoww, Mr. Vinci had a lady friend, did 'e?" I supposed, trying to keep from smiling. This caused them all to laugh again, and tut-tut about my education. Little did *they* know...

"Perhaps, but Mona Lisa was not his 'lady friend,' as you put it," Mr. Cambridge continued. "In fact, no one is certain who she was. But she is very plain—not pretty at all."

"It is her smile that makes her unique, I should say," Mr. Wilder decided.

"And Miss Lisa is coming to London?" I asked.

"No one knows that for certain, either," Mr. Cambridge said regretfully. "You will have to wait and hear about it after the opening!"

This set them to talking about who had been invited again, and I knew I would get no more out of them. Besides which, I knew that the Gold sisters would be arriving within the next ten minutes, and I had to prepare another pot of tea.

E

ANOTHER HOUR PASSED, and dozens more patrons entered before I heard more about the "oil" that I suspected to be the one Jack meant. If it truly had given someone the "slip," it was not yet common knowledge. At least not this early in the morning.

Jack did his bookwork at his high desk—I cast glances at him through his office door as he busily wrote in the ledger, counted order slips, and double-checked the inventory. But I knew he was listening to every wisp and tendril of conversation he could catch, and locking it in his memory. Once he finished, he rolled up his sleeves and came out to help me juggle the morning rush, which filled the house with noise and steam and the scraping of chairs, and which left me amazed that neither he nor I sent a single tray careening onto the floor. Neither of us ever had to write down orders, even for the requests of the most finicky customers—we were too sharp and too experienced to forget anything. Well, except when Mary walked in.

Jack was in the middle of taking another request for tea from Miss Jane Gold, one of our favorite well-to-do old maids, when Miss Mary Moore swept into the coffee house like a summer breeze. I paused, my hands full of empty mugs, and watched Jack straighten, abandon his duty and stare at Mary as she floated in, wearing a new white spring dress, light blue jacket and white hat. She sent a lovely smile to everyone in the room who turned to greet her, and reached up to unpin her flowery bonnet.

"Good morning!" she said breathlessly, her cheeks flushed from the chill outside. "It's a beautiful day, isn't it?"

Everyone heartily agreed with her—even the center old gentlemen who had complained so bitterly about the weather before. Mary has soft brown hair and eyes, a flawless complexion and a winsome figure—the most beautiful young lady I have ever seen. Not only that, but she has such an engaging smile and bright disposition that no one in the coffee house can say a disagreeable word about her.

Jack went straight up to her to take her jacket, while Miss Jane lifted a hand in protest and tried in vain to finish her order. Mary greeted Jack with a bright glance and smile, and let him take her jacket, then swept to the front of the room where I stood.

"Good morning, Miss Else," she greeted me warmly. "I love the way you have pinned your hair today."

"Thank you, miss," I replied, smiling and dipping into a quick curtsey as she then passed by to open the door to her manager's office. Jack trailed after her, walking right past me as if I were not there, still carrying her jacket, his eyes fixed on her. I sighed and shook my head, and attended to Miss Jane myself. Why did this behavior always catch me off guard? It happened every morning.

E

MR. MCDOUGAL STILL had not come in by eleven that morning, and I was getting impatient. I still had heard nothing concrete about the "oil" Jack had hinted at, which made it even worse. I was certain his suspicions had something to do with the traveling show—one that had been kept so secret, and the invitation list so selective that not even affluent art-lovers like Mr. Cambridge had been invited. And Jack would tell me nothing—he was helping Mary with the ordering. Perhaps that is why I made my first mistake in six months and walked a full tea tray right into a gentleman's chest.

It crashed to the floor, shattering the tea pot and saucers and cups and creamer and sugar, and spilling the hot liquid all over me.

"Oh, Miss! I am so very, very sorry!" the young man exclaimed. I gasped and leaped back, blushing so hard it hurt, seeing that I had also spilled down the front of his white shirt and dark suit. His wide blue eyes found mine.

"Please forgive me—it was entirely due to my clumsiness," he said hurriedly. "I was not paying sufficient attention to—"

I did not bother to listen—I dove onto the floor to pick up the broken shards. I felt the eyes of the entire patronage on me, and heard their muttering. I moved more swiftly to pick up the glass—

Pain bit my right index finger. I yelped and jerked my hand back to see bright red liquid bloom from a cut in my skin.

"Oh, this is all my fault," the young man lamented, kneeling down before me. "You've hurt yourself."

"Aaow, it ain't nothing, sir—I should 'ave been watching meself closer," I said. "Begging your pardon, sir."

"No, no—let me help you," he insisted, and began picking up the pieces. I winced, and tried to help with my uninjured fingers.

"What happened?"

I heard Jack's voice overhead. I shot to my feet, holding my wounded hand.

"Sorry, sir—I spilled me tray. This kind gentleman is 'elping me—I begged 'im not to—"

Jack searched my face worriedly before masking it and facing the young man.

"Really sir—do get up. The staff will take care of that."

"*I* will take care of it," Mary strode up beside Jack and gave him a reproving look. "Can you not see, Mr. Young? Miss Else has hurt her hand."

Jack glanced at me. He *had* seen it, but the rules must be followed...

Mary took hold of my arm and steered me to the only empty booth.

"Sit down, Miss Else, and I will get you a bandage. Sir, if you would sit with her and see that she is well? I will get you a towel."

"Thank you, miss, I will surely do that," the young man, smitten with Mary's vivacity as everyone always was, nodded quickly and slid in across from me. I squeezed my fingers down on my wound, but it only bled more.

"Oh, here—use this," the young man offered, holding out a white dress handkerchief.

"Thankee, sir," I said, and took it from him, then bound it around my cut. I glanced up at him, taking the opportunity now to study him closer. He had neatly-combed blonde hair, clear blue eyes, and strong features. He was well dressed, in country style. He looked a little shaken. I gave him a sideways grin.

"No need to fret, sir—'appens to me all the time."

"Oh, forgive me—I did not ask to be introduced," he sat up straight. "My manners are terribly lax today."

"Me name's Elsie Jones," I answered. "But everybody what comes in here calls me Miss Else."

He gazed at me a moment, then smiled slowly.

"Well, I hope you will forgive me for my lapse, and for causing such a mess. I'm afraid my thoughts were rather distracted."

Out of the corner of my eye, I saw Mary and Jack cleaning up the tea mess and pretending they were not eavesdropping. I kept my attention on the stranger.

"This is a good place to sort out one's troubles, I've 'eard," I commented. He shook his head and sighed, settling back in the booth and brushing at the tea stain on his shirt. I laughed.

"Most of the time, anyhow," I added. "When one ain't getting tea thrown at 'im!"

He chuckled, then shook his head again.

"I believe you, Miss Else—however, I'm afraid nothing can set my mind at ease today."

"Someone ill?" I asked. He halfway smiled.

"No, thank God. But this situation is a great deal more complicated, and I am afraid I cannot discuss it. Unless..." He narrowed his eyes at me. "Miss Else, may I ask you a question? A question you certainly need not answer if you do not wish to."

I waited, keeping my expression pleasant and open. He sat forward, bracing his elbows on the tabletop.

"You doubtlessly hear quite a bit of nonsense as people come in and out of these doors, do you not?"

"Oh, yes, indeed," I chuckled. He remained serious.

"Have you, perchance, heard any nonsense concerning a painting?"

I hesitated.

"I 'ave 'eard the gentlemen talk about a show of Da Vinci paintings coming to the Smith and opening tomorrow night," I said. "But I just today knew who Mr. Da Vinci was."

His voice lowered.

"Have you...perchance...heard a rumor about one of them disappearing?"

My eyes went wide.

"Being stolen, you mean?"

"I didn't say that," he said quickly. "Just...missing."

I frowned.

"No, sir," I bluffed, then softened my gaze and let it sparkle. "Not until just now."

"Oh, I beg you not to repeat that," he urged me, placing a warm hand on my forearm for an instant. "For if it is only a rumor, I would be most grateful not to have it spread. I myself have only heard it from a single source, and therefore it may be empty."

The little chime on his pocket watch sounded, and he reached into his pocket and eyed the time.

"I hope you will forgive me, Miss Else, but I was on my way to an urgent appointment when I bumped into you. I must be on my way."

"Don't trouble yourself, sir," I said as he got up. He watched me for a moment as he put his pocket watch back.

"You seem like a good sort of girl—I hope I haven't gotten you into trouble."

"Thankee, sir—I'll manage," I replied.

"I certainly hope so. Good day."

"Thankee, sir," I said again. "Good day."

And he left me with his ruined handkerchief, and more information to process than I had time for at the moment. I only knew, as I got up to find out where on earth Mary had gone with the bandages, that I needed to have it processed long before Mr. McDougal came in.

E

THE GREAT CLOCK OUTSIDE struck two, and the patrons of the coffee house filed out, leaving the place empty. Closing at two o'clock for an hour had been a tradition for a hundred years—one that I was most grateful for. Otherwise, those who worked here would have no chance to eat, or sit down for more than two minutes together.

However, this hour-long tea break served a more important purpose.

No sooner had Jack locked the front door than Mr. George McDougal burst in via the back way, his green velvet coat draped over his elbow, his hat in his hand, and his face flushed. Mr. McDougal is the owner of this business—a bold Irishman with auburn hair and blazing green eyes. He is a hearty, athletic, good-looking gentleman perhaps ten years my senior. I paused while picking up five cups from a table, and watched him march straight toward the staircase.

"Up, up!" he called. And that instant, Mary, Jack and I broke from our work and filed after him, casting glances to make certain the place was indeed empty.

I trailed after Mary's white hem up the spiral staircase. The stairs creaked beneath our weight—my good hand slid along the cool iron banister. In no time, Mr. McDougal reached the top landing and I heard the jingle of his keys as one of them rattled in a lock. Then, the upper door swung open, and Mr. McDougal, Jack, Mary and I finished climbing and stepped into the place Mr. McDougal calls the "Crow's Nest."

Mr. McDougal was a seafaring man in his youth, and therefore feels the need to call up memories of it often, but it really is a fitting name for this spot. Tall windows with small, square panes face the east—the side of the Oxford, and one can see down onto the street from there, and over quite a few rooftops. *If* one can manage to see past all the clutter in the room.

This small room, once meant to be an office for the proprietor, does have a desk, but that is where the similarities end. In this room, books are piled in stacks from the wooden floor to a height taller than Jack—books of languages, maps, potions and poisons; classical architecture, old-English riddles, music, and Russian Czars; locksmithing, ciphers, navigating, handwriting and chemistry; etiquette, religion, tattoos and lists of the most famous thieves, murderers, pickpockets and con-men who ever lived.

Beakers, vials and test-tubes lined one counter, while a fingerprinting kit littered another. A large table sat in the center—clear, as it always was for each new beginning. And around it stood a long couch, and two tall-backed cushioned chairs—one with red upholstery, one with green. Everywhere, one can catch glimpses of the marks of our personalities, and interests and profession.

For this room is us. Just as this coffee house shows a bustling, working-class front to the public and yet secretly holds a veritable library of crime-detecting knowledge, so I work as a waitress, Jack as a clerk, Mary as a manager and Mr. McDougal as the owner—yet I am a dialect and language expert with a photographic memory, Jack is a mathematician and architecture and cipher authority, Mary is a proficient of people-reading and hypnotism, and Mr. McDougal is a walking trove of history information and a connoisseur of all art and literature. These skills are vital to not only our job but sometimes our lives—for we work for Scotland Yard as their finest and most select detective agency. And so far, no one but a handful of people knows that.

I sat down on my customary side of the couch and leaned against the armrest, still favoring my now-bandaged hand. Jack flopped down at the opposite end, sighed and ran his fingers through his hair. I kept my eyes on Mary as she daintily moved to the red chair and settled down into it.

"Please tell me you distracted that young man into running into me, Mary—or I will have to take drastic measures," I said, dropping my cockney like a heavy bag and glaring at her. Her eyes twinkled and she leaned toward me.

"Tell us about him."

"Not until you tell me *why* you made him run into me without letting me know what you were doing," I shot back. "I have a cut on my finger now because of you."

"We want to hear your unbiased opinion, Elsie," Jack said. "We didn't want you to have any ideas about him before making your assessment."

"Yes, please give as much detail as you can, Miss Jones," Mr. McDougal said, leaning his elbows on the back of his chair and watching me with those emerald eyes. "That way I can find out for certain if all of this mayhem that Mary and Jack have created is going to be helpful or not."

"It very well may be, Mac," Mary insisted, glancing at him. "But I refuse to say anything until Elsie does."

I gritted my teeth, then sighed at their expectant looks.

"Very well. The initials on his handkerchief were E.M. He is young—perhaps twenty-five. From his dialect, I gather that he is from Surrey, in the town of Horley. Well-bred, with a mother from Wales. He is a Cambridge graduate, and has spent some time in the Americas—perhaps the West Indies. He is not accustomed to conversing with ladies."

"His father died when he was young," Mary chimed in, with facts she had gleaned with her own skills. "He has easy country manners, but he is a gentleman at heart—his mother married up, and therefore had a better understanding of the hardship of the lower classes, which transferred to a sympathy on her son's part toward those less fortunate than himself. He did not distinguish between Elsie and me in terms of treatment—in fact, he was genuinely concerned with Elsie's welfare, rather than looking after her because I asked him to."

"His coat is of the latest fashion, and custom-tailored, and his shoes are hand-made," Jack said. "He is very well-off."

"Besides which, he seemed to want to start the rumor that one of the Da Vinci paintings had been stolen," I finished. "Either that, or make certain it already *had* been started."

Mr. McDougal nodded once.

"Interesting. Especially since it is not a rumor."

I sat up straight. Jack's gaze flew to McDougal.

"So it is true? What I overheard last night?"

"Partly," McDougal said, coming around his chair and seating himself. "The place is sealed up tight as a drum—they are not even allowing officers from Scotland Yard inside yet, protesting that the other paintings are not ready to be exposed—however, I managed to learn only three things from a museum guard. Three very intriguing things."

Mary narrowed her eyes at him.

"It was not a Da Vinci, was it?"

McDougal just smiled to himself, quite used to her penetrating insight. I, on the other hand, gaped at her.

"*Not* a Da Vinci?" I repeated.

"She is right," McDougal nodded. "The painting that was stolen is called 'A Young Patrician Lady'—and it was painted by one of Da Vinci's pupils."

"Who?" Jack asked.

"No one knows," McDougal replied, folding his hands and resting them on the tabletop. "Neither do they know *when* it was painted. It is a beautiful portrait, but not so famous as so many of Da Vinci's works.

Which brings me to another intriguing fact I learned." McDougal leaned forward and met all our eyes in turn. "The 'Young Patrician Lady' was hanging next to the 'Mona Lisa.'"

"Why wouldn't the thief take *that* instead?" Jack wondered.

"Too recognizable," I guessed. "Too hard to sell."

"So sell it as a forgery," Mary suggested. "A good copy is very valuable, and if the thief picked a rich, ignorant buyer, no one would know the difference."

"A thief would have known that," Jack said. "He would not have taken a painting by a nameless man who merely copied Da Vinci's style. Not if he could have the Mona Lisa"

"And therein lies the mystery," McDougal declared. "Enough of a mystery that Scotland Yard wants us on the case. Especially considering the *third* fact I uncovered."

We all leaned forward.

"Officer Humphrey, one of my good friends as you all know," McDougal said. "Told me that all of the windows and doors in the Smith are iron-barred, and they bolt shut from the *inside* only. The guard who locks them stays the night there."

We waited. Mr. McDougal looked at Jack.

"Not a single bolt was thrown that night. Every single window and door was found bolted shut in the morning. Nothing was broken or tampered with. And the guard heard nothing."

I glanced at Mary. She almost looked excited. I felt the same way, but kept it from my face.

"We need to know what kind of thief we are dealing with—for he is certainly no ordinary thief of antiquities," McDougal said. "That is where you come in, Jack."

Jack sat up.

"What do you need?"

"I need you and Elsie to study these while Mary and I take over your duties in the coffee house this afternoon." McDougal got up and pulled out some sheets of paper from inside his coat and laid them out on the table: the first scraps of paper that marked the beginning of a case. I leaned forward, gazing at them.

"Blueprints."

"Circa 1800," Jack said, his keen eyes roving over the straight pencil lines and tiny writing. "I would say...1802. Yes, here is the date. Skylights, wide, airy hallways, two stories, a huge storage basement..." he glanced up at McDougal. "This is the Smith Museum."

"It is indeed," McDougal nodded. "Get to know it like the back of your hand. Tonight, you and Elsie are going to break inside."

E

IT WAS DARK WHEN JACK met me beneath the sallow light of a weak lamp on our designated street corner. He no longer wore his smart coat and hat. This time, he had donned a ragged set of clothes and a flat, brimmed hat, with a scarf to pull close to his face. I wore similar rags, with trousers beneath my skirt, a woolen coat, a beaten straw hat and a scarf as well. He strode up to me through the inky fog, his heels on the stones the only sound—I was not alarmed. I knew his footsteps by heart.

"'ello, luv," I greeted him, lifting my head so he could see my face. "Fine night for a stroll, eh?"

"Don't tease me, Elsie," he muttered, keeping his voice very low. "You know I am no good at dialects."

"Which is why Mac wanted me along, I s'pose," I smiled. "I'm not much good for anythin' else."

"Oh, tosh," he scolded, then hopped up on the curb and offered me his right arm. "Shall we?"

I smiled again, and took hold of his arm, and we stepped swiftly into the darkness, leaving the lonely pool of light behind.

We swept through the dark, dirty streets, fog swirling around our ankles. Far away, the haunting bell of Big Ben sounded the stroke of two. I kept close to Jack, for it was a damp, chilly night. We said nothing.

We soon abandoned the main roads and ducked into a twisting alley where only the meager moonlight could penetrate from straight overhead. A cat skittered away from the sound of our passage and disappeared around a corner. Our feet stepped surely around waste bins and fallen bricks—we knew these alleys like the backs of our hands.

I squeezed Jack's arm in warning. He glanced down at me. I lifted my head to indicate the black silhouette of a short man in a battered top-hat lurking in one of the doorways ahead. Jack put his hand over mine.

"'ere, who's that?" the dark man asked, his voice low and gravelly.

"'ello, Jim," I called out, matching the exact dialect used in these particular wretched alleys. "Just out for a walk with me sweetie is all."

"Bessie May, is that you?" Jim straightened, and the growl vanished from his rough voice. "A bit late out for courtin', ain't it?"

"Aoow, the moon is a fine thing tonight!" I responded as we strolled past him. I caught a glimpse of the patch over Jim's left eye and his scraggly beard. He watched us go.

"You 'ad best get inside, luv," he advised. "It ain't safe—not 'ere, it ain't."

"Thankee, Jim—we'll be careful," I assured him as he vanished into the darkness behind us. As soon as we were out of earshot, and around another filthy corner, Jack leaned close to my ear.

"Bessie May?"

"Yes," I answered. "One of my aliases down here."

"Ah."

We kept walking, watchful but at ease, for acting like a courting pair was a masquerade we had adopted many times. Jack thought nothing of it. I was not sure what *I* thought of it.

At last, we stepped into a section of London that was not so disreputable—it was like passing from night into day. The streetlamps burned brighter, the streets were clear and clean, and I heard the *clip-clop* of a mounted bobby as he rode down the center of the cobbles. Finally, after two more twists and one more turn, we reached our destination:

The back alley of the Smith Museum.

The Smith towered over us, its great dome blocking out the moonlight. The buildings closed in over us. I winced. I never enjoyed that caged feeling.

I sensed him before I saw him: a man pressed against the only door back here—the barred back door.

"Scotland Yard. Who goes there?" came the quiet, inquiring voice as the man caught sight of us.

"Twist the knob and bend the key," Jack replied.

"Ah. I wondered if you were coming after all," came the much more-relaxed reply.

"Good evening, Humphrey," I greeted him. "Lovely night."

"Right," he muttered. I peered at him as best I could in the nearly non-existent light. A dim shaft of light flashed against the silver badge on his helmet as he turned to face us and dug in his pocket. Keys jingled.

"I would not have done this, not for one moment, if I didn't owe Mr. McDougal such a vast debt," Humphrey grumbled. "I left the Smith guards with a good reputation—it got me my post on the force. So if either of you *touch one thing*," he jabbed his finger at us. "I will make certain your heads are on pikes right next to mine."

"Don't worry, Humphrey," Jack soothed. "We'll not trouble you for more than fifteen minutes of your time. And we swear we will not touch anything."

"I will hold you to that," Humphrey warned as he opened the barred door. A vast, dark space opened up before us. Jack and I bent down, took off our dirty shoes, tied their laces together and hung them over our shoulders, then stepped in our stocking feet onto the hard, cold marble.

"Be quick! You are now on the clock," Humphrey said, and Jack pulled me forward into the blackness.

E

"I CANNOT SEE," I WHISPERED, clinging to Jack's arm as we swept blindly down the cold, dark passage.

"Then listen," he breathed. "Remember the blueprints, listen, and orient yourself. Hear how our words and steps echo, but not greatly? We are in a marble hall with a curved ceiling, but no skylight. There are no paintings on these walls, nor office doors to dull the sound—we are merely walking down a hallway that leads out, in case of a fire. Remember?"

"Yes. Now I do."

We kept walking, and as always, it was as if Jack could see in the dark. He never got lost in a building, even if he was blindfolded. *"Listen, listen,"* he would often say. *"Listen, and you will find out infinitely more than if you speak."*

"Hello—here we are," Jack said, and pointed ahead. I could see him point ahead, because in the ceiling of the room beyond was a skylight that captured the moonlight and filtered it down to coat everything in silver.

"This is the dome," I said as we stepped out into the perfectly circular beam of main light. Both of us stopped and looked up. Jack nodded.

"Yes—look at how steeply it curves down, with no ledges at all. And the circular skylight up there is less than a meter wide in diameter—I would say seventy centimeters. Curved glass on top, sealed in place."

He kept gazing at the dome while I turned from it and glanced at the paintings hung on the walls of the circular room. There was the Annunciation, the mysterious Mona Lisa—

And between it and the Portrait of Cecilia Gallarani was a blank space.

I stepped closer. I could see where a painting almost the size of the Mona Lisa had been hung, by wires and hooks meant to keep both the painting and the wall undamaged. I stood in front of that blank space, studying it, wishing I had brighter light.

"We have established that the thief did not get in and out through any of the windows and doors, correct?" I said, canting my head as my eyes were drawn to Mona Lisa's mysterious smile. The portrait's eyes seemed to gleam, as if she knew something we did not. I smiled myself. She certainly did. *She* had seen what had happened the night of the burglary. If only she could speak...

"That is the way it appears," Jack said. "But it may not be true."

"What of the skylight?" I pointed out, coming back to walk into the beam of moonlight and gaze at the towering dome. "Could he have come in that way?"

He frowned up at it.

"Perhaps. If he knew how to remove the glass without breaking it, and had ropes with which to climb down—"

"Jack."

I froze where I was, staring up at the skylight.

"What?" he said, and quickly stepped up beside me.

"Look."

He did. And he saw exactly what I saw.

It had been hidden before by our angle, and the silver of the pale moonlight. But now, from where we stood, we could clearly see a small white feather hanging by a thread from the edge of the skylight. In the daytime, it probably would have blended right in with the white of the surrounding walls.

"That is a calling card. It *was* the skylight!" I breathed. Jack suddenly frowned, then spun around.

"What is it?" I asked. He stared at each of the paintings, and then the space between the Mona Lisa and the portrait of Cecilia, and I could see that he was measuring something critical.

"The paintings are each exactly half a meter apart from each other," he noted, his keen eyes darting. "Which would make the Patrician Lady..." He whirled around and stared up at the skylight. "Far too wide."

"What are you saying?" I demanded, my heart beating faster as we both stared up at the ghostly white feather.

"The thief could have gotten *in* by way of the skylight," Jack said. "But if he was carrying the painting..." He looked at me. "It would be impossible for him to have gotten *out*."

CHAPTER TWO: "Inside Information"

As told by:
JACK YOUNG
London

April 10th, 1890

THIS CASE HAS TAKEN an unusual turn. I always look forward to thrills and forbidden investigations of crime scenes, no matter how often they happen. But it has been a while since I have been totally baffled.

I stood there on the marble floor in my stocking feet next to Elsie, staring up at the small white, moonlit feather dangling by a thread from the edge of the skylight. Calculations flew through my head—calculations so numerous and complicated that I did not have time to explain them to her, even if she could understand them. Elsie, however, cut into my thoughts with a penetrating question.

"What are you saying, then? That, since the thief could not have gotten it out through the skylight, the painting is still in the museum?"

I blinked.

"That is a possibility..." I supposed.

"But why would someone do that?" Elsie asked. "Take the painting down and hide it?"

"Perhaps to come back later and take it out by another, easier route," I guessed. "But the feather puzzles me. Why would a thief deliberately leave a clue behind?"

"Because he is arrogant," Elsie answered. "He thinks he has already succeeded."

I glanced at her, seeing a smile cross her face at the foolishness of that thief—

And then I heard footsteps echo through the dome.

"The night guard," I hissed. Elsie whirled toward the sound, but I grabbed her elbow and hauled her back the way we had come.

Our feet pattered against the stones, quiet as cats' paws, as we raced like shadows into the dark hallway.

I heard Elsie panting—used the sound of it bouncing back from the walls to judge the distance to the exit. I felt the draft of outside air—I stretched out my hand and pushed against the door, felt it give way—

And pulled Elsie through the gap and into the alley. Humphrey shut the door right behind us, almost catching Elsie's hem, and locked it.

"Find anything useful?" he inquired.

"Something interesting, anyway," I admitted, out of breath.

"Good. Then I bid you goodnight," Humphrey said, clearly still miffed, and turned and marched away, twirling his club as if he was merely out pounding a beat. I shook my head, bent and put my shoes back on. After she had done the same, I turned to Elsie.

"Shall we?" I asked, and offered her my arm. She nodded, saying nothing. I knew she was thinking. And for the rest of the walk home, neither of us spoke—mostly because it was dangerous to make one's presence known this late at night, but also because the memory of a single white feather filled both of our minds.

J

WE WERE FORCED TO WAIT until the break at two o'clock the next day until we could discuss our discoveries with our colleagues. Mr. McDougal had opened in the morning so that Elsie and I could recover, but we still came in at nine. Elsie was short-tempered from her lack of sleep, and I was irritable with impatience. We snapped at each other more than once before Mary came in.

"Good morning, Jack!" Mary greeted me, as happy and brilliant as ever. The slight headache I had felt before vanished at the sight of her in her light yellow muslin dress, and I felt altogether restored when she beamed at me.

"Good morning, Miss Moore," I answered, the noise and clatter of the patrons around me fading into the background. She glanced around at the crowd of customers as she pulled off her hat.

"Has Mr. McDougal come back yet?" she asked. "I know he went walking after you and Miss Else relieved him—I strolled with him for a bit before coming here."

"No, he's not here," I answered. "And so I would greatly appreciate *your* help with some of the orders."

She smiled at me again, and nodded.

"Certainly."

Mary and I retreated to my office to discuss the ordering of more beans, and we left the Gold Sisters in Elsie's capable hands—they always preferred her to wait on them, anyway.

As I sat down on my high stool and bent over my ledger, I could literally feel Mary's impatience—it was almost as strong as my own.

"Did you learn anything last night?" Mary came around and whispered into my left ear, keeping me between her and the open door so that no one could see what she asked.

"Yes," I answered, keeping my eyes fixed on the numbers I was writing.

"Well, *what,* for heaven's sake?" she pressed, though she still whispered. "You *must* tell me—I have been in an agony to know."

"I cannot tell it now," I protested, though I would like nothing better to reveal it all to her at once and watch her face light up at my narration.

"Why not?" she demanded.

"Because there is too much," I answered, glancing up at her bright brown eyes. I had to look away, then, or she would take away all my resolve. "I'll tell you everything when Mr. McDougal gets here—and Elsie can add her theories as well."

Mary sighed, but I refused to give up any more, and she turned to helping me with inventory.

When Mr. McDougal blasted in, however, both of us dropped our pencils, raced to the exit and held the doors open for the customers, almost urging them to leave more quickly. Elsie cleared away the last of the empty mugs, and then we all leaped up the stairs into the Crow's Nest. Mr. McDougal had barely locked the door behind us before Elsie and I were speaking.

"Humphrey let us in, there was no problem—"

"We went right down the hall into the new gallery with the dome—" I said.

"It was all very dark, except for the skylight—"

"And we found the space where the Patrician Lady should be—"

"Sit down, sit down," Mr. McDougal cut in, holding up his hands to pacify us. "One at a time, please."

Elsie and I sat down on the edge of the couch, and I could tell Elsie was gritting her teeth waiting for Mary and McDougal to take their seats. McDougal sighed, draped his coat over the back of his chair and sat down, running his hand through his dark hair.

"We have a need for expediency now, for the fact that the Young Patrician Lady has been stolen has now hit the front page of the papers," McDougal said. "The entire town is abuzz—and the thief knows the jig is up. It would be brilliant if either of you have found something with which to track him before he is chased out of England by all this publicity." He glanced at Elsie. "Miss Jones, please tell me if you encountered anyone last night," he asked, his ever-keen, calm eyes focusing on her.

"Only Jim Hale, in his customary alley; and Humphrey," Elsie answered.

"Did you speak to Jim?"

"As I always do," she replied. "He warned us to be careful, walking through town so late at night."

"And how was Humphrey?" McDougal wondered, and I caught the trace of a mischievous smile as he spoke.

"Cheerful as usual," I replied, answering the smile. McDougal chuckled, sat back in his chair and folded his arms.

"Very well. Tell me what happened."

I glanced at Elsie, who nodded at me, and so I began. I told Mary and McDougal how we had spotted the place where the Patrician Lady used to hang, and how we noted the width of the portrait, and the diameter of the skylight. They listened, absorbing every detail. Then, when I paused, McDougal turned to Elsie.

"Was there any hard evidence left behind, besides the obvious fact that the painting was missing?"

"Yes, sir," Elsie nodded. "A white feather hung from the skylight."

McDougal stared at her. Then, he shook his head once.

"That's not possible."

"That is exactly what I said," I leaned forward. "The width of the painting and the diameter of the skylight make it impossible to—"

"No, Jack," McDougal met my eyes—and I went still.

"What?" Mary frowned, watching him. McDougal sighed and gazed down at the blueprints on the table, but his face looked distant.

"The white feather. It is a calling card."

"That is what I assumed," Elsie added.

"But it cannot mark the exit route," I protested. "The thief could not physically get the painting out that way."

"Oh, the thief that left that kind of calling card certainly could," McDougal revealed, his voice low. "He could make the painting disappear entirely, and then reappear in his drawing room half an hour later." He paused. "Except for the fact that he is dead."

I glanced at Mary, but her eyes were fixed on McDougal.

"You knew him," she said. McDougal nodded.

"I saw him die."

Silence fell as we waited for him to elaborate, but he did not. So much of McDougal was open and honest—and I trusted him with my life—but there was still so much of his past, before I knew him, that was shrouded in darkness. Although he had just turned thirty-seven, he seemed to have lived an age. The mark of all he had seen was that moment written in his eyes, and none of us could decipher it.

I heard Elsie take a breath.

"So...the one who left a feather—he could be an imitator of this great dead thief," she suggested. "Someone meaning to intimidate the police force and lead them down false trails."

"Perhaps," McDougal said quietly, still lost in thought. "Although he would have to be a fool to dare imitate *him*, even after death..."

"That leaves us with only two options, then," Mary stated. "One: The ghost of this fantastic thief has whisked the painting off to his cobwebbed castle somewhere, *or*," she looked at me. "The robbery was an inside job."

"That occurred to me as well," Elsie said. "Especially after our friend Humphrey was able to let us in so easily. What's to stop the night guard from letting his own friend in?"

"What would the guard gain?" I frowned.

"A bribe," Elsie answered.

"At the cost of his job?" I protested, then shook my head. "Once the curator found out that a priceless painting had been stolen the night before the grand opening, that guard's head would be on the chopping block."

"Perhaps it was more than bribery," Mary guessed. "Perhaps he would obtain a cut of the sale of the painting?"

"What guarantee would he have that the thief would deliver after he had escaped?" Elsie prompted.

"The guard could always turn the thief in," McDougal said. "After all, the guard would know enough about the thief to give the police as many clues as they wished."

"And don't forget," Mary reminded us. "This still leaves the question: Why did he not take the Mona Lisa?"

"We need to know more about the security of the museum," I said. "We need to know all about the guards, where they are stationed, and who was on duty that night."

"Where would we get that information?" Mary wondered. McDougal smiled at her. Elsie sighed.

"Mary—it looks as if you are going to a party tonight," she said.

"Oh, wonderful!" Mary cried, turning her brilliant eyes to me. "And of course I must take Jack—I will never remember all the ins and outs of the hallways on my own."

McDougal addressed me.

"Jack, you have a black suit, do you not?"

J

OF COURSE I HAD A BLACK suit. And Mary, I was sure, had recently purchased the latest fashions. But right at the moment, that was not our worry.

Our worry was the invitations.

So far as we could discover, none of our patrons had received an invitation to the Da Vinci grand opening—not even Mr. Cambridge, who used to be a professor of art. All four of us prodded and prompted each of our customers, which was easy enough to do because the gala was the talk of the town, but not one could produce an invitation. And no matter how clever we were, Mary and I could not get into the grand opening and move freely without that piece of paper. Not this time.

Mary drew near me where I stood in the corner drying a mug with a rag, and both of us gazed out over the customers.

"Their disappointment and confusion is so thick it almost chokes me," she murmured. "Sometimes I wish I did not understand everyone so well—it gets tiresome."

I glanced down at her, disconcerted. But the next moment, her troubled expression vanished as she caught sight of someone coming through the door. I lifted my face to see Elsie escorting a middle-aged bespectacled, primly-dressed lady and her friend to a booth. It was Mrs. Sprig, the owner of the bookshop down the street, and Mrs. Afton, her favorite coffee companion.

"Do you see that?" Mary whispered. "Do you see how Mrs. Sprig smiles, how she walks?"

"What about her?" I asked, trying to see whatever-it-was that Mary always seemed to spy when reading people.

"She is happy—quite satisfied," Mary said, a slow smile spreading on her face as she watched the two ladies. "She has just received something in the mail that she liked very much, that made her feel included and important. Mrs. Sprig?" Mary left my side and swept right up to Mrs. Sprig and Mrs. Afton's table. I followed at a distance, watching.

"Good afternoon, ladies!" Mary greeted them, clasping her hands in front of her. "Miss Else is getting you your coffee, I presume?"

"Good morning, dear!" Mrs. Sprig answered, the lamplight glinting off her spectacles. "Yes, Miss Else has helped us already."

"Hello, Mr. Young!" Mrs. Afton caught sight of me. "Good day to you!"

"Good day," I nodded my head.

"And how are the two of you today?" Mrs. Sprig's eyes twinkled as she glanced back and forth between Mary and me.

"Lovely," Mary answered breezily. "Although we are quite disheartened to hear that no one of our acquaintance received an invitation to the Smith Museum this evening!"

"Aaoow, but Miz Sprig's got one," came Elsie's voice at my elbow, and I glanced down at her. She met my eyes for a moment before carrying the coffee tray to the ladies.

"She told me so 'erself right when she come in."

I fought to conceal my admiration. Elsie could not read people as well as Mary could, and her personality was a great deal rougher, but no one could accuse her of being lax in her detective work. Not for an instant.

"Do you indeed?" Mary cried to Mrs. Sprig. "Oh, may I see it? Is it beautifully done?"

"Done by hand, I believe," Mrs. Sprig filed through her purse, lifted out an envelope and card, and held it proudly out to Mary. Mary carefully took it, and I saw her run her soft fingers across the paper, feeling its texture, and I watched her eyes canvas every detail of letter and design.

"It certainly *looks* as if it was done by hand, doesn't it?" Mary mused. "And what lovely gold edges it has! When did you receive it?"

"Only today," Mrs. Sprig gingerly took it back from her and put it away. "I certainly did not expect to receive one—but then again, my nephew recently took a position as one of Mr. Messini's assistants. Mr. Messini is such a gracious employer—perhaps this is a reward for my nephew for performing his duties so well!"

"Mr. Messini?" I repeated. Mrs. Sprig turned to me.

"Oh, yes, he is the new curator, and owner of the museum."

"I have heard his name," Mary said. Elsie retreated out of the circle of our conversation and stood just behind me, listening.

"Will Mr. Messini be there?" I asked.

"Oh, I do hope so," Mrs. Sprig said. "He is a delightful Italian man—I have only met him once, but he has the most genteel manners."

"I certainly hope you enjoy yourself," Mary smiled at her. "You must come and tell Miss Else all about it tomorrow!"

"I certainly will!" Mrs. Sprig promised. Then, as Elsie distracted the ladies by asking about their cream and sugar, Mary turned and took my arm.

"Come, Jack. We have invitations to print."

J

DID I EVER MENTION in this journal before that Miss Mary Moore is an expert on all forms of forgery? Well, even if I have, it is worth repeating, because she amazes me on a weekly basis with her talent. Mere moments after we raced up to the Crow's Nest, leaving McDougal and Elsie to deal with the customers (with McDougal's blessing, of course), Mary leaped behind her desk, which was covered with all sorts of inks and dyes and stamps. As I watched, she opened a right-hand drawer and flipped through several types of paper, drawing a few of them out and feeling them.

"It looked like vellum paper, didn't it?" she mused. I shrugged.

"I suppose...?" I watched her a moment more. "Do you need my assistance?"

"Yes, unfortunately," she muttered, finally drawing a large piece of paper out. I jolted with disappointment. Then she glanced up and saw my expression. She laughed.

"No, that is not what I meant!"

"What did you mean, then?" I asked, relieved in spite of myself.

"I meant that Mrs. Sprig's eyes aren't as good as they used to be—or the light in the coffee room is far too dim. That invitation was *not* hand written."

"Why did you tell her it was?" I asked. She smiled.

"The same reason Elsie speaks as if she were a flower girl."

I watched, and waited, as Mary set up her little printing tray, carefully selecting the correct style of letters, and the proper arrangement. Then she rolled the carefully-chosen ink across the letters, swiftly and expertly.

"Now, Jack, I need you to roll this press across the paper *twice*, strongly and evenly. You have a better angle, since you are so tall," she said, then set the paper where it needed to be and got out of my way. Biting my lip, I took hold of the handles of the roller, pressed down, and rolled it over the paper, once forward, once backward. As soon as the roller cleared it, Mary swiped the paper out of the printer and held it up to look at it. She grinned.

"Brilliant," she decided. "Looks and feels almost exactly the same, if I do say so—now all that is left for this one is the gold edges, and then I will make yours."

"Let me see," I requested. She handed it to me, and I read it.

Miss Mary Moore
is invited to attend
The Smith Museum's Da Vinci Collection Grand Opening
and be among the first to view
More than fifty paintings belonging to
The great Renaissance master
And some of his pupils
on Friday, the tenth of April
In the year of our Lord Eighteen-hundred ninety
from seven in the evening to eleven in the evening
The Smith Museum
London
Wine and cheeses will be served
No admittance without invitation

I WINKED AT HER.

"Genius, Miss Mary."

Her grin never faded.

"Thank you, kind sir."

J

THE EVENING FELL SOFT and bright, and the streetlights of London glowed like candles in a church. Mary and I rode in her coach and four through the crowded streets, and as we rode, I listened to the musical *clop-clip* of the horses' hooves and the chatter of the wheels against the cobbles. I glanced across at Mary, who was decked out in a beautiful white formal gown and gloves, and smiled.

"Did I tell you that you look lovely tonight?"

She sent me a sparkling look.

"Thank you, Jack—you look dashing, yourself." She reached up to touch the back of her braided bun. "And I appreciate your compliment, especially when I spent nearly an hour on my hair. It simply wouldn't cooperate."

I gazed at her a moment longer before turning to the window.

"I am certain that you vex half the population of London by the fact that you swear you will never marry."

"I may vex them, but I do not vex myself," she replied lightly. "Marriage chains one to a parlor and a dining room and a nursery—how on earth could I be of any use to you and Elsie and Mac if I were married?"

"Perhaps your husband would not object to your work," I ventured.

"Ha!" she laughed. "Show me a man like that and I will poke holes in him, for he would certainly be imaginary."

I watched her pretty face as she gazed out of the window, sadness in my heart. But she did not notice my mood—or, more likely, she did not address it—because when she faced me next, she changed the subject.

"Do you know who Mac meant when he spoke of that brilliant thief?" she asked, her tone quiet and serious. "He has never spoken to me about it. But I can tell by looking at everything about him that there is more to the story than Mac merely bringing a criminal to justice. Much more."

I shook my head and sighed.

"He's never told me about it, either. And I doubt he will, even if I asked him."

Trouble crossed Mary's brow, but the next moment, the carriage drew to a halt, the footman hopped down and opened the door for Mary. He helped her out, and then I climbed down and offered her my arm—

And we stood on the curb, gazing up at the magnificent, lit façade of the Smith Museum. Dozens of other couples, all equally well-dressed, stepped out of their own coaches, which now formed a great long line in the street in front of the museum. The music of a stringed quartet issued from the open front door, as did the sounds of many people walking, talking and laughing.

"The invitations must have merely been issued late," I murmured to Mary.

"It doesn't seem as if the party is so exclusive after all, does it?" she agreed. "Well, good. Easier for us to blend in."

We climbed up the stairs—Mary fairly floated—and we handed our "invitations" to the uniformed man at the door.

"Thank you so much for coming," he smiled to us as he handed them back. And we strolled through the front door without a hitch, just as I had known we would.

The entrance hall of the museum was all illuminated with the new electric light, which made it shine brilliantly, and lit up the paintings as surely as daylight would. It was filled with people milling around, enjoying cheeses, wines and champagnes, and gazing at the art that hung up on the white walls, or the marble statues that populated the floor. Beyond the crowd stood two towering double doors: the grand entrance to the new gallery.

I recognized many of the faces of the guests and museum staff alike, and they also recognized us. We were greeted warmly, and often, by people young and old. We mingled easily, Mary appearing to follow my lead even as she guided me with the subtle pressure of her fingers upon my arm. For just as I was I was recognized as *Elsie's* "sweetheart" by the folk of the gutter, I was known as *Mary's* beau by the folk of high society. And while excursions with Elsie often brought the adventure I so enjoyed, the outings with Mary gave me the chance to be by her side, and bask in the warmth of her smiles. Even if she never did save a special smile for me.

I instantly noticed the moment she caught sight of something important. She hesitated, and her brilliance faded to an expression of focus.

"Jack," she murmured. "There is Mr. Messini, the owner."

"Where?" I asked, scanning the crowd ahead of us.

"Talking to that young lady in blue," Mary answered. "Come on."

Together, we threaded our way through the guests, and at last arrived at the side of the museum owner and curator. He was a short man, with black hair and a mustache; darting black eyes, prominent nose, and an expensive starched suit and tie. The moment we arrived, he glanced at us, and the lady with him sensed she had lost his attention.

"Excuse me, I must rejoin my party," she said, curtseyed, and departed. Mr. Messini turned to us then, and searched our faces. I knew he was trying to decide whether or not he recognized us.

"Mr. Messini!" Mary cried pleasantly, offering her gloved hand. "We were so thrilled to receive your invitation! It was so gracious of you to think of us again."

"Oh, 'tis no trouble, madam," he answered, taking her hand and forcing a smile. I tried not to show my amusement. The poor man had no idea who we were—but he was embarrassed to admit it, because Mary was so confident.

"Good to see you again, Mr. Messini," I said, extending my own hand. "We always look forward to your openings—my own art collection is extensive, but there is nothing like gazing at a wall covered in the great works of one of the masters."

I saw something in his expression change—a camaraderie entered it, the mutual understanding of fellow art-collectors. I felt Mary's fingers on my arm and hid my smile. She had taught me well.

"Yes, yes!" Mr. Messini shook my hand. "So glad you could come."

"So, are the rumors true?" Mary asked. Mr. Messini blanched.

"Rumors?" he choked.

"That there are paintings within the new show that belong to Da Vinci's pupils, as well as those of the master himself," Mary added, watching him.

"Oh!" he cried, pulled out a white handkerchief and dabbed at his neck. "Oh, that! Oh, yes that is true. It should be a treat for all of you to see them."

"Indeed," I nodded. "We are looking forward to it. But it seems," I ventured. "That you thought Miss Moore meant something else. I apologize. We did not mean to remind you of the stolen painting."

"Oh, yes," Mr. Messini sighed. "You need not have worried—for I am reminded of that every moment since it happened!" He dabbed his face now. "I am most distressed. That painting is priceless, even if it was only done by a pupil of Da Vinci. And the fact that it was stolen from under our noses is now all over the front pages of the newspapers, and it is the talk of the town. I have been so preoccupied by that disaster that I have hardly been able to enjoy the opening." The man wilted. Mary put a soft hand on his elbow.

"I am so sorry," she said gently. "I certainly hope it makes a reappearance."

"Oh, so do I," he nodded. "Very soon!"

"How were you able to repair the damage done by the burglary in time for this event?" I prodded. The curator shook his head woefully.

"That is what is most upsetting, sir. There was no damage! It was as if it floated away on its own wings."

"Incredible!" Mary exclaimed. "No window was ajar? No lock broken?"

"Nothing at all!" Messini cried, throwing up his hands. "As I said, it is as if it flew away. The guard heard nothing, and nothing else was taken. No window or door was left open a crack!" He sighed again. "It does not look as if any evidence can be found, even by Scotland Yard's best. I despair of the painting ever returning."

"But I don't understand—why would someone steal *that* one?" Mary wondered. "Especially if several of Da Vinci's own paintings were nearby?"

"Ah, you see, this is why I thought you mentioned rumors," Mr. Messini muttered. "It seems that there is a rumor traveling through artistic circles that, hidden within the painting, are clues to a great Doge's treasure buried somewhere beneath the streets of Venice." He shrugged heavily. "I do not know if these rumors are true, but perhaps the thief was willing to take that risk!"

Mary and I exchanged a glance. But before we could say any more, Mr. Messini jumped, and reached into his pocket to pull out his watch.

"Good heavens, it's time. Please excuse me." He bowed to us, then hurried through the crowd toward the double doors. We followed him swiftly, wishing to be among the first to pass through the doors.

"When everyone is distracted by the paintings," Mary whispered to me. "We can make our way to a few of the guards and ask them about their shifts, and who was on duty last night."

I did not answer, for Mr. Messini stopped, turned around and clapped his hands, and the roar of the crowd died down.

"Ladies and gentlemen, welcome to the Smith Museum!" he shouted, and his voice echoed through the large room. "I am honored to receive you tonight, and hope that you are equally honored to stand before some of the greatest masterpieces ever created. It is time now to open the doors—time now for you to step into the presence of a genius. Enjoy yourselves, ladies and gentlemen. I give you Leonardo Da Vinci, and the works of some of his finest pupils."

With that, he waved his hand, and two assistants stepped up and opened the great, heavy doors. They heaved open, revealing the now fully-lit circular room that Elsie and I had invaded the night before.

The cry went up before I saw it. Mr. Messini lost all color, and put a hand over his mouth. Mary clamped both hands down on my arm. I just went stiff.

I blinked several times, to be sure I saw what I saw. But there was no mistaking it.

There, between the Mona Lisa and the Portrait of Cecilia Gallarani...

Hung the portrait of "A Young Patrician Lady."

CHAPTER THREE: "Suspicious Ties"

As told by:
Miss Mary Moore
London

April 10th, 1890

THE CURATOR HAD BEEN lying—constantly lying. I could not pinpoint exactly what he was hiding as Jack and I spoke with him, but I *did* know that the dismay he expressed over the loss of the Patrician Lady was not real.

However, everything changed when those doors swung open to reveal the missing Lady right where she should have been: between the Mona Lisa and the portrait of Cecilia Gallarani.

This time, the curator's reaction was genuine. I watched him go pale, watched him stare at that reappeared painting as if it were a ghost. Interesting. Instead of rushing forward in joy and relief, he gaped in horror. As if something had gone terribly wrong.

I smiled.

"Jack," I whispered. "Quickly." And I pulled him forward through the throng.

The crowd rushed into the room, their loud comments and eager questions running over each other as they pressed up to the painting.

"Quick, quick!" I urged Jack as we wove through. I pulled him toward a darker side corridor, counting on *him* to remember where we had come from and where we were going. He was the one who had memorized the blueprints, after all.

"We must hide," I hissed.

"What?" Jack cried, looking back. "Why?"

"To get what we came for!" I jerked him around and pulled him even further down, using the chaos out in the main gallery as a smoke screen. Then, I pulled him into a recessed doorway, and we pressed our backs against the closed door.

"Mary, what are we—" he started.

"Wait and see," I whispered. We could just see the edge of the colorful, bustling crowd through the doorway far down the hall. Moments later, just as I had predicted, Mr. Messini's voice rang out over the crowd.

"Ladies and gentlemen, please! May I have your attention? Please? Ladies and gentlemen, I am afraid you must leave immediately. As you can see, the stolen portrait has reappeared, and therefore I *must* contact Scotland Yard. Please understand—you may be treading on evidence at this very moment!"

This excited the crowd rather than calmed them, and I bit my lip to control my laughter.

"They don't want to leave," I told Jack. "But he'll make them."

"How do you know?"

"Just watch."

"Guards, please show my guests out," Mr. Messini called. I gripped my hands together and fought to stay still.

Many protests ensued, and questions, but the guards won the struggle, and the guests reluctantly began to file out, leaving us quite alone.

Almost.

I sensed his presence just an instant before I saw him. I whipped my head around to peer up the dark hall—

To see a figure dash away around a corner.

"Jack!" I hissed.

"I saw him!" he answered, and broke into a run. I hiked up my skirt and hurried after, knowing I was taking my life in my hands by running in heels on this slick marble floor.

"*Confound* this dress!" I cursed as Jack's dark form pulled away from me and whisked around the distant corner. My shoes clattered against the tiles—I thanked God that the noisy crowd behind me could muffle my racket.

I skidded around the corner, fighting to keep my balance—

To see Jack catch our quarry, grab his arm and fling him into the corner. Jack raised his fist.

"Stop!" I cried. Jack froze, then took hold of the man's collar and looked at me over his shoulder.

"What is it?"

"Don't we know you, sir?" I gasped to the stranger, stepping closer. Indeed, I was certain I was not mistaken: I recognized the combed blonde hair, handsome face and striking blue eyes. The man, his hands raised, glanced at me, and his eyebrows went up.

"Er...I believe so?" He stammered. Then he suddenly smiled. "I know I've seen that lovely face before."

Jack shook him hard.

"Stop, Mr. Young," I commanded Jack. "Don't you remember? This gentleman was a patron in our coffee house just yesterday."

Jack stared at me, and then a light came on behind his eyes. He instantly released the stranger—for he knew the look I was giving him: if we acted as agents of Scotland Yard before a man who was barely a suspect, our covers could be blown.

Jack cleared his throat, then straightened his own tie.

"Forgive me, sir—I'm afraid Miss Moore was frightened when she saw you in the hall," Jack said, his face still stony. "After seeing what had happened with the portrait, I was acting to protect her, and the other guests."

"It's quite all right," the young man nodded, pulling his own collar back into place and watching Jack carefully. "I understand completely."

"But I still must know why you were hiding in the hallways, and ran from us," I pressed, coming closer. The young man glanced between us.

"First of all, let me introduce myself properly. Edward Manchester, at your service." He held out his hand to Jack. Jack paused a moment, then shook it. Mr. Manchester smiled at me.

"I'm sorry to have startled you, madam—I was skulking in that corridor because, strictly speaking," His brow furrowed. "I am not supposed to be here."

I canted my head, then exchanged a glance with Jack.

"Indeed?" I said. Mr. Manchester clasped his hands behind his back and shook his head.

"I was not invited—I sneaked in with some of the guests—not to do any harm, mind you. You must hear me," he said earnestly. "I was just so concerned—I wanted to speak to Mr. Messini in person earlier today, but he refused to grant me a meeting. You see, that painting, the Young Patrician Lady, belonged to my father, God rest him." His eyes grew sad. "It was his very favorite. And when I heard the earliest rumors that it had been stolen, it shook me to my core."

"You only heard rumors? Why would the curator not tell you immediately if your property had been stolen?" Jack wondered. Mr. Manchester looked at him.

"I don't know. That is one of the reasons I came so quickly. That painting has incredible importance to me—Messini should know that! My father had a large debt to repay—the sale of the painting was to go toward payment of that debt. Mr. Messini told him he could find a buyer for it easily. And then it vanished."

"But it has reappeared!" I pointed out, purposefully infusing my voice with excitement and a little endearing silliness. "What do you think of that?"

Mr. Manchester glanced at me with increasing warmth—exactly what I wanted.

"I can't believe it," he admitted shaking his head. "It is incredible. I stood there staring at it for I don't know how long. And I could not help but wonder..."

Jack's eyes narrowed.

"Wonder...?"

Mr. Manchester gave him a grave look.

"What did the thief mean by taking it and then putting it back?"

I smiled to myself. I had my own theory, but I wanted to hear Jack's first.

"Perhaps he thought he was getting too much attention," Jack supposed. "Lost his nerve."

"But he was so tricky in the way that he took it and then put it back—it is fascinating!" I pointed out, folding my arms. "It's as if he were a ghost."

"I wouldn't suppose a man like that would be nervous about a few headlines," Mr. Manchester surmised.

"Perhaps it's a threat," I said. Mr. Manchester regarded me now with admiration.

"You think so?"

Jack scowled.

"That is an intriguing idea, Miss Moore," Manchester said. "Perhaps the thief means to show Mr. Messini that he can come and go at will, and take whatever he wants. Perhaps it is extortion."

"You mean..." Jack frowned at him carefully. "He wants Mr. Messini to pay him to *not* steal paintings from the museum?"

"Well, it makes sense to me," Manchester said.

"But how would Mr. Messini know that's what the thief wanted?" I asked. Mr. Manchester's gaze drifted back the way we had come, and he grew pensive. I watched him, unblinking.

"Perhaps..." he mused, then met my eyes. "Perhaps he left him a message of some kind. Something in his office?"

"In that case, he will certainly tell Scotland Yard of it," Jack decided—and I could tell that he had decided we were speaking too freely. "And Messini will also tell Scotland Yard about *us* if we keep loitering around in dark hallways."

"Let him," Mr. Manchester lifted his chin. "Then at least I will have his attention! In fact, I have a mind to march right into his office this moment and give him a piece of my mind."

"Oh, do let us tag along!" I begged, giving him my sweetest smile. "I'm dying to know more about this—and I'm certain that tomorrow my patrons will ply me with questions about it!"

Mr. Machester thought for a moment, then nodded.

"Certainly. Do come with me. Perhaps he will be more inclined to listen if there are more of us."

Jack shot me a questioning and irritated glance, but I just smiled and took Mr. Manchester's arm as he casually offered it, and the three of us trotted back down the hall toward the signs that indicated the offices.

Now, *this* was engaging. Manchester *wanted* us to come along. But why? Why would he want two virtual strangers, and coffee-house owners no less, to accompany him to a personal meeting concerning his father's art? Oh, this was definitely worth following—I was sure of it.

"There," I pointed to a large, ornate white door—the last one in the long line of them. It hung slightly ajar, and bore Mr. Messini's nameplate beside it. Our footsteps slowed, and I released Mr. Manchester, who hesitated.

"Mary..." Jack cautioned, but I ignored him. I pressed my fingertips to the door, pushed it open further just a hair, and glanced inside.

A single lamp burned on a meticulously-organized desk. Otherwise, the room was dark, and abandoned.

"He is not here," I said.

"Shall we wait for him, then?" Jack suggested, and I knew he meant to have a look around for himself.

"Shall we?" I gave a smile to Mr. Manchester, who looked nervous. He smiled back at me, and together, the three of us filed into the office.

"It does not appear as if he ever enters this room, does it?" I said, glancing around at the tall, shadowed bookshelves, perfectly arranged, the shut doors of the coat closet in the opposite corner, the two chairs before the desk that looked untouched, and the surface of the desk itself with a stack of paper to the left below the lamp, an inkwell to the top right, and sealing wax to the top center.

"He does come here, though," Mr. Manchester noticed. "Look at the ash tray. It needs to be emptied. And I smell a Cuban cigar."

"Ah, you're right," I nodded, spotting the ash tray on the other side of the inkwell. Our shadows, thrown by the flickering light of the lamp, played like murky reflections against the gray walls. I frowned down at the desktop.

"No message in the obvious place," Jack observed.

"What about the behavior of this thief has been obvious?" I murmured, frowning as I cast my gaze back at the door. I cocked my head. "A man so particular about the state and order of his office would certainly lock its door when he left it, don't you think?"

The two men turned, and stared at the door through which we had come.

"Yes," Mr. Manchester said. "Indeed he would."

Silence fell. I heard the ticking of a small clock, and glanced up to see one hanging above the door of the coat closet.

"Miss Moore," Mr. Manchester started. "What if—"

"Shh!" I grabbed his wrist. He went still.

"What is it?" Jack whispered, leaning toward me but staring at the door.

"Someone is coming," I said through my teeth. "Listen."

For a moment, all was quiet. And then...

Distant footsteps clicked down the hall somewhere. Two sets. And then a man spoke.

"There is nothing convenient or beneficial about this, Mr. Richards! It is completely intolerable!"

I bit my lip, and my heartbeat accelerated. It was Mr. Messini and his head guard, Mr. Richards.

"I'm sorry, sir," Mr. Richards' deeper voice replied. "But I fail to see how the return of the portrait could be distressing to you—"

"How can you not?" Mr. Messini burst out. "I am being toyed with! This thief is taunting me, acting as if he can come and go as he pleases. For all I know, it may be gone again tomorrow!"

"Perhaps you should contact Mr. Edward Manchester and relieve his mind—I am certain he has been grieved by the theft of his father's painting—"

"To blazes with Manchester," Mr. Messini growled—and his footsteps gained speed and force. "It is his fault this has happened—*he* was the one who began all of this treasure mischief. He has humiliated me in front of all my peers, and the artistic community." His voice lowered, but I heard what he said next: "If I saw that meddling whelp this moment I would cut him down."

I gripped Mr. Manchester's wrist tighter, my blood going cold. I heard a new layer in Mr. Messini's voice—one I had not sensed before...

My breath slowly left me as my instincts solidified into truth:

We were in danger.

My gaze flew to Manchester's, and locked there. His

eyes went wide, and he swallowed. I clamped my jaw.

"Continue on your rounds, Richards. Pursue it if you see *anything*—he may still be inside!" Messini commanded. Now he was just down the hall.

"Get in the closet," I urged, and without waiting for a reply, I pulled Mr. Manchester toward Mr. Messini's coat closet, opened it and pushed him inside, shoved the long wool coats back, then grasped Jack's hand and pulled him in as well.

"Mary, you really must tell me what—" Jack tried, but I shut the door on us, locking us in pitch darkness, except for the narrow slit of lamplight that filtered between the doors. Mr. Manchester stood crushed against my right side, and Jack stood crushed against my left. The wool coats pushed against our backs and the tops of our heads, and I made a face. I *detest* wool!

I could hear the breathing of the two men—I wished they would be quieter. But I dared not shush them, for the next moment, the door of Mr. Messini's office slammed open.

Jack and Mr. Manchester stiffened. Heavy steps betrayed Mr. Messini's hurried entrance. He muttered something I could not hear, and moved toward us. I gritted my teeth and held my breath.

He passed us. A drawer whipped open—he was at his desk. He pulled something heavy out—something heavy and metal that slid like a snake against the bottom of the drawer...

And the distinct, thick, repetitive *clack* of a handgun being locked and loaded filled the room.

My heart clenched and my face went cold. Mr. Manchester slid his hand down and gripped my fingers. Jack bent over me. I closed my eyes and tried to listen, even though my pulse now roared in my ears.

Mr. Messini muttered again, then kicked aside his chair, which rolled. He stopped. He said something in Italian—something quiet and questioning. Then, paper rustled. He tore open an envelope. He paused. Then, he spoke again in Italian, though this time the word was harsh, like a curse. He dropped the paper—not far, just to the desktop. Then, he swept out of the room and slammed the door behind him.

None of us moved for a full minute. At last, Mr. Manchester relaxed, and released my hand. I drew in a shaking breath.

"How on earth did you know we needed to hide, Miss Moore?" he murmured, his voice low and solemn. I shrugged.

"Woman's intuition," I said weakly, pushing the door aside. I could not help my squeamishness—I *also* detest *guns*. I am unlike Elsie in that regard—she is a great proficient with firearms. I imagine that, if she had heard only what I had, she would be able to tell everyone what kind of pistol Messini had, and what caliber bullet he had loaded. Just thinking of it made me ill.

"This is madness. Utter madness," Manchester whispered, covering his mouth with his hand.

"Why did he say that about you starting the treasure mischief?" I asked him. He swallowed.

"I gave him the information about the possible clues in the painting that would lead to a Doge's treasure—I wanted him to mention it to buyers, to increase the chances of it being sold." He glanced down. "Doubtlessly, he now blames *me* for the fact that it has now become the prey of thieves."

"Mary?"

Jack had spoken. He had moved ahead of me, and now glanced back at me, holding up the piece of paper Mr. Messini had found.

"Where was it before?" Mr. Manchester asked.

"Must have been on the seat of the chair," Jack mused. I took the paper from him and held it toward the lamplight, studying every pen-stroke, every edge and surface of the paper. I read the words aloud.

"AS YOU CAN SEE, I HAVE returned it. You may
inspect it all you wish, but you will find that
it is the genuine article.
I hope this causes you as much distress as you
have caused me with your lies. I am most displeased.
You cannot fathom the resources and efforts your
dishonesty has cost me. I expect compensation—
nay, I demand it. I will meet you in your office
at the stroke of midnight to discuss terms.
If you do not appear, I will have to find another way
to deal with you."

I glanced at Jack.

"It isn't signed. But I can tell the personality of this man by his penmanship."

"Can you?" Mr. Manchester laughed uneasily, shifting closer.

I almost winced. I kept forgetting I needed to keep up my guard.

"Oh, it's a hobby of mine—a little science I study for amusement," I said, flashing him a smile. "See? He writes with heavy pressure. This means he expends a great deal of effort and energy when accomplishing all his tasks. He is patient, with a long memory. His writing slants to the right—his heart is his monarch, rather than his mind—although it does not slant *so* much. His mind is still quite active, and he listens to reason. But this loop atop the 'o' is interesting."

"Why?" Manchester wondered. I met his blue eyes.

"It means he has secrets to keep."

"Mary, we must go," Jack urged. "There is no telling if that mad curator will be back—and I certainly do not want you anywhere near a *gun*."

"Believe me, I do not *want* to be anywhere near a gun, no matter the quality of gossip at the Oxford tomorrow," I told him. "Mr. Manchester, will you walk with us? I think you had better forget about speaking to Mr. Messini—and I cannot bear the thought of you alone in here, especially with that insane man angry with you."

"Certainly, thank you," Manchester nodded, and together, we opened the door and edged out into the dark hallway, leaving the letter right where we had found it.

We saw nothing but shadows as we swept back down the hall toward the dome, my skirts rustling, darting from dark corner to dark corner, begging the Almighty to mask our passage.

And He did. Until we reached the center of the darkened dome gallery.

"I see you!" Mr. Messini howled from behind us, his scream hammering through the room like thunder. "You cannot escape this time!"

"Run!" Jack roared, and yanked me forward into a small side hall. We threw aside all caution and pelted into the blackness. Mr. Manchester's feet pounded on my left, Jack's on my right.

And then a gunshot banged down the hall. I screamed and threw my hands over my ears. Plaster exploded from the right wall and struck our heads. We kept running.

Jack leaped forward, slammed his shoulder into the short door ahead of us and wrenched it loose of its lock. Mr. Manchester gave it a sharp kick, and it snapped open enough for us to break through and out into the chill London air.

"Go, go!" Jack cried, grabbed my arm and hauled me down the moonlit alley. My good shoes splashed through cold puddles. My breath hitched in my chest as I kept running as hard as I could, the buildings flashing past. I felt faint, but I would not let myself lag. I had to keep up with Jack and Manchester.

The echoes of our footsteps gained hollowness. We wove through several streets and back alleys, fleeing half a mile before we paused beneath the weak glow of a street light. It was then that I turned, panting for dear life, and realized that Edward was gone.

"Where is he?" I gasped, my eyes going wide as I searched the shadows. "Where did Edward go?"

Jack, drawing himself up, gazed back into the darkness. His jaw tightened.

"Just as I thought."

I frowned at him.

"What?"

"I'll tell you later," he said, steel in his eyes. "We need to talk to McDougal."

M

I SAT WRAPPED IN A blanket, my wet shoes off, my legs tucked up beneath me, my vanilla cappuccino curled in both hands, and my chair tucked up next to Mac's within the warmth and safety of the Crow's Nest. Mac's green eyes now captured mine for a long moment—for Jack had just told him of the gunshot that had chased us out the door. I gave Mac a shaky smile, but he just gazed at me. My smile faded. Even with all my skills, I could never hide anything from him.

Mac cleared his throat, then rested his elbow on his armrest and draped his fingers over his mustache.

"Theories?" he asked.

Elsie sat up, and light flared to life behind her serious blue eyes.

"Mr. Manchester is the thief."

"It's obvious," Jack nodded, glancing at her.

"Wait—what?" I almost spilled my drink. "*Edward?*"

"Why are you calling him by his first name all of a sudden?" Jack demanded, his cheeks flushing. I stared at him.

"Jack, there is no time for that right now."

"No time for what?" Elsie cut in. "It's perfectly clear. Manchester *knew* about the Doge's treasure, and stole the painting back to look for the clues. Then, Manchester replaced the portrait and was retreating when you caught sight of him. Once Jack seized him, he could either confess to being the thief, or pretend to be an innocent victim; try to win your sympathies so you would forget how suspicious he had just been acting. You must also consider the fact that he was *very* quick to tell you his entire story—the tragedy of his life." Elsie arched an eyebrow. "As if he had rehearsed it for just such an occasion."

"Not to mention that he completely disappeared as we were fleeing," Jack pointed out. Indignation flooded me.

"Either that or he became *lost* while we were speeding through all those God-forsaken streets," I snapped.

"Impossible," Jack shook his head. "We could not possibly run fast enough to lose him—not with you and that dress in tow."

"I resent that."

Mac rested his warm hand atop mine for a moment. I bit back my next words and set my teeth.

"Stop feeling and start thinking," Mac rebuked us. "No one can deduce without a clear mind. Take a moment to breathe, then align your thoughts."

I watched as the fire behind Elsie's eyes dwindled, replaced by cool consideration. She propped her elbow on the table—which now bore the blueprints, the invitations, and a copy of the note left to Messini, which I had remembered and written down.

Jack did not relax as much as Elsie did, but he folded his hands in his lap and cast his gaze down. Mac raised his eyebrows.

"Now," he started. "What Elsie and Jack say make a great deal of sense. But for some reason, Mary's instincts do not lean that direction." He met my eyes. "Care to explain?"

I glanced at him, then sighed.

"Edward—Mr. Manchester—is a good man. And I know this because I did not feel the need to keep my guard up. I found myself thinking aloud in his presence—and I would *never* do that unless I knew in my heart that he is not a villain. Think of it! If he did steal it to look for clues, how could he have searched the painting thoroughly so quickly? And if he *did* find something, why would he leave a threatening note?"

"An interesting thing, that note," Mac murmured, his cool eyes resting on the piece of paper. "It does sound as if the thief was expecting something, but did not find it."

All of us fell silent.

"And another interesting point," Elsie murmured. "Why would the thief send Messini a note like *that,* as if Messini had inconvenienced him?" She met my eyes, and held my gaze. "As if it was somehow Messini's fault..."

A suspicion began in the back of my mind—and when I glanced at Mac, and saw a twinkle in his emerald eyes, it was confirmed. A smile started on my lips.

The small wall clock chimed. We all glanced at it. It read half past eleven.

"There you have it," Mac declared, as if the discussion was over and a conclusion had been reached. But none of us questioned him—none of us were lost. We understood, and we rose to our feet.

"We have half an hour to ready ourselves, get word to Humphrey, and get across the threshold of the Smith," he said. He buttoned his coat, and winked at me. "Let's be quick!"

CHAPTER FOUR: "The Appearance of Things is Deceiving"

As told by:
Mr. George McDougal
London

April 11ᵗʰ, 1890
MIDNIGHT

"ARE YOU SURE ABOUT this, sir?" Humphrey asked me, his breath a cloud of vapor in the moonlight. He brushed at his mustache, then raised his eyebrows. I glanced at him, then back at the crooked back door of the Smith museum. I straightened my tie, then put a hand to the revolver that hid at my hip under my coat.

"As sure as I am about anything, Free," I answered, using my old nickname for him. "Watch my back."

"Right behind you," he said, then yanked open the door. It groaned on its crooked hinges, and I gave a half smile. The poor door would never recover. Jack didn't know his own strength.

I stepped over the threshold, and took a deep breath. I smelled the gunpowder from Messini's weapon, fired a little more than half an hour ago. My heels clicked on white, polished marble as I strode forward. Humphrey fell in behind me, matching my steps. Judging by the echoes, the hall was fifty meters long. I entered the domed gallery, and the vastness and quiet of it opened up above me. I spotted the Young Patrician Lady, hanging just where she ought to be, and tipped my hat to her. Then, I continued straight on, down the black corridor toward Messini's office, recalling the blueprints as if I had them in my hands.

Keeping my eyes forward, I waved Humphrey off, and he fell back, halting by the entrance to the corridor. I turned the corner, slowed, stopped, and listened.

For a moment, I heard nothing. Then, the sound of two masculine voices reached me. One belonged to a young man; well-bred, calm. The other belonged to an older man, bearing an Italian accent that had been eliminated from the hearing of all but the most experienced ears. I glanced up.

Messini's office door hung open

I stepped forward on the quieter leather of my shoes, keeping my heels from clicking, and pressed my back against the wall next to Messini's half-open door. I slowed my breathing, then held it, and listened as the two men inside stepped closer to the center of the room and began to speak again.

"Do you have any idea what this errant venture has cost me?" the young man said, his tones low and tight.

"So take the painting and sell it—it will bring you a good price, and you may keep all of it, instead of my usual fee," Messini tried. I sensed his masked desperation—he held it in check by keeping his volume low.

"That was not our agreement," the young man countered. "Besides, why would I take *that* when I could have a Da Vinci?"

Messini paused.

"You wouldn't dare."

I heard the young man fold his arms.

"Oh, I wouldn't?"

"If you took the Mona Lisa, I would be ruined," Messini growled. "No collector would trust me with his art anymore—and no thief would respect me."

"You should have thought of that before you fed faulty information into the black market in hopes of a quick profit," the young man said flatly.

I leaned sideways, ever so slightly, and eased my head around just enough so that I could see into the room with just one eye.

There, in the center, illuminated by the flame of one oil lamp, stood Messini—still in his black suit from the gala—and a taller, black-clad, hooded man with a bandana over his nose and mouth. They faced each other squarely. The young man stood with feet apart, arms crossed. Messini, however, held his hands to his sides, clenched into fists. His eyes blazed at the other man.

"I warn you, I will have your head if you so much as touch one of the other pieces," Messini snapped.

"You are lucky I do not take *your* head this moment," said the young man.

"You would need more than your own hand to take my head," Messini snarled.

"Perhaps I have more at my disposal," the other man said. "Perhaps—"

I pushed the door open. Messini shrieked. I jerked back out of the way—

Just as he whipped out his gun and fired through the doorway. I flinched, the shot ringing in my ears. I yanked out my own handgun, cocked it, swung around and fired straight at the floor at Messini's feet. He leaped back, then leveled his weapon at me again. I spun back and took cover around the doorframe. Shots rang out, bullets biting into the opposite wall. Smoke filled the air.

A hand touched my shoulder. I glanced to my right—Mary stood there, pressed against my wall, beside Jack. Jack held his own weapon up by his ear. I glanced across the doorway.

There waited Miss Jones, her own sleek handgun resting in both hands as if she was cradling a cup of tea, her bright blue eyes watching me. She wore all white—her best dress. She held my eyes and nodded. Dark, helmeted forms waited behind Miss Jones' shoulder—Humphrey, and two other bobbies.

I glanced back at Mary. Her brown eyes met mine, and her fingers closed around my elbow. I could feel her fear, even though she hid it from everyone else. I gave her a warm look, the one I reserved only for her. She swallowed, nodded, and returned it. Again, I looked at Miss Jones. She lifted her chin. I took a deep breath.

"Scotland Yard!" I roared. "Drop your weapons and you will not be harmed."

"Of course you are," Messini retorted with sarcasm. "Just more thieves and brigands! If you come through this door I will pin you to the wall."

"I am sure you would. If you had a gun. Kindly drop it to the floor."

My head whipped around and I stared at Mary. That was the thief's voice! And then...

The sound of a revolver striking the carpet thudded through the room.

"Feel free to come in now, officers," the thief announced. "You're quite safe."

I put my right hand down and squeezed Mary's fingers, cautioning her. I eased an eye around the doorframe once more...

The thief stood, arm outstretched, pointing a small handgun to the back of a very pale Messini's head. I wheeled around the doorframe and pointed my own gun at the thief's heart. Instantly, Miss Jones, Jack, Humphrey and the other officers followed me, raising their own weapons.

"Oh, no, there's no need for that," the thief held up his hands, set his own gun down on the desk, pushed his hood back, pulled down his mask...

To reveal a flushed, handsome face, slightly-mussed blonde hair and bright blue eyes.

"Edward?" I heard Mary's voice cry out from behind me. He laughed, and ran a gloved hand through his hair. Mr. Messini whirled on him, his eyes wide as saucers.

"Manchester?!" he yelped. His whole face turned red. "Why, you...You bold faced liar! Give me an inch and I will—"

"You will stay calm, sir, and kindly be quiet," I said, pointing my gun at him. "Please."

I thought for a moment that Messini might suffer an aneurism—he puffed and grunted so hard, and sent me a most hateful look—but finally he bit his lip, and fell silent.

"Humphrey, if you would?" I said. Humphrey grinned at me.

"Certainly, sir," he stepped forward, spun a baffled Messini around, and handcuffed his hands behind him. Another policeman scooped up Messini's weapon. I lowered my gun. So did Elsie and Jack.

"What—What is this?" Messini demanded. "Am I being arrested?"

"Yes," I said frankly. "For shooting at officers of Scotland Yard, for one—and for laundering paintings to thieves for another."

"This is outrageous!" Messini roared. "You cannot prove anything! And I did nothing but defend myself!"

"Certainly," I nodded, and gave him a bright smile as Humphrey and one of the other policemen hauled him out of the office.

I felt Mary come up to my left, Jack stood beside her, and Miss Jones waited just behind my right shoulder. I faced Mr. Manchester. He was still ruddy, and quite pleased with himself.

"Now, sir, I believe you have some explaining to do," I said. I glanced at Mary, who was watching him intently.

"I believe you came to the Oxford Coffee House not a day ago—and you also met Miss Moore and Mr. Young at the gala just earlier this evening," I reminded him. Manchester chuckled again and folded his arms.

"Yes, that was indeed me," he said, his eyes brilliant. He laughed out loud, then shook his head. "Forgive me—I am still just astonished that it worked!"

I considered him for a moment, pieces clicking together in my mind, and then I gave a small laugh of my own.

"Ah," I breathed. *Now* I understood.

"If you would enlighten us, I'm certain it would be helpful," Jack said, his tone still black. I suppressed a smile, made certain that both Miss Jones and Mary were eyeing Manchester keenly, inclined my head to Manchester and gave him an opening.

"Please, sir. It would behoove you to tell us what you were doing masquerading as the thief."

"Oh, I was not masquerading," Manchester's eyebrows went up, and his expression was both eager and open. "I *was* the thief."

Mary, Miss Jones and Jack froze—and then we all waited in silence, listening. Manchester grinned. I was tempted to return it. He had followed the lead I had provided—the final proof I needed—and it all made sense, now.

"Well...All right," Manchester conceded. "Seeing as you have all done me a great favor, I will certainly tell you."

"Please do," Miss Jones said. "At the beginning."

Miss Jones' curtness could not stifle Manchester's incandescent satisfaction. He halfway sat on the edge of Messini's desk, clasped his hands, and began to speak.

"Years ago, my father lent Mr. Messini, an old and dear friend of his, six Da Vinci paintings for a tour—Father had spent a fortune acquiring them," he said. "When Mr. Messini reported that they had all been stolen, my father was crushed. He invested a great deal of money and effort trying to recover them—private detectives, police, even bounty-hunters." Manchester held out his hands, palms up. "Nothing turned up for years, and my father, discouraged, took sick." The smile faltered on his face. "As I am sure was obvious—for it has caused great turmoil in my family—I was *greatly* opposed to my father's decision, but nevertheless, he decided to allow Mr. Messini to show and sell his last great piece: 'A Young Patrician Lady.' Then, my father died, and I was forced to auction off all his other artwork to pay his debts. But only the sale of the Patrician Lady would eliminate the debt. Then, one of my father's old detectives came to me with a discovery: the thief who had taken my father's work was known as the White Feather."

My mirth faded as that name fell from his mouth. I swallowed, and a chill crossed over my skin.

Don't be foolish, Mac, I told myself. *Dead is dead.*

"I began to track this thief," Manchester said, an edge of iron entering his voice. "It took me a few years, but I finally began to piece together clues that proved that he stole from specific museums in five different countries—museums connected in some shape or form with Mr. Messini."

Out of the corner of my eye, I saw Mary and Jack glance at each other. Miss Jones kept listening, never wavering. Manchester met her intense gaze for a moment, then went on.

"I supposed the White Feather stole from Mr. Messini because Messini is famous for collecting and displaying the finest art in Europe. I began to learn the White Feather's methods, and I got closer and closer to discovering his true identity."

A frown tightened my brow, and deep, unsettled cold settled in my gut. I folded my arms over my chest. Manchester took a breath, and met my eyes.

"And then I received word that an Irish inspector by the name of McDougal had discovered the White Feather's hideout and taken him down."

Mary looked at me, and edged closer to my shoulder. I did not look at her. I stared back at Manchester. He sighed.

"I was comforted in *that*, at least—even though my father's paintings were not recovered." He glanced at Jack. "But then, not a month later, one of Messini's museums was robbed. The thief was caught." Manchester paused. "It was *not* the White Feather. And the artwork had already been sold."

"So you knew it was not the White Feather who was entirely at fault for the loss of your father's paintings," Jack surmised. Manchester nodded.

"Yes. It was then that I became suspicious of our old friend, Mr. Messini."

"Is that the laundering you spoke of, Mr. McDougal?" Miss Jones said to me.

"Exactly," Manchester said, pointing at her. "The suspicion grew in my mind that he was *allowing* the thieves to take the artwork in exchange for a fee, and a cut of the sale. But I needed proof. I had to set a trap."

"And you began by inventing a treasure," I said. Manchester smiled.

"I sent a letter to Mr. Messini, telling him about the mythical Doge's treasure and its connection with the Patrician Lady. Then, I used what resources that remained to me to listen through the black market. Sure enough, the information I had given to Mr. Messini was leaked into circles of thieves."

"You could not allow anyone else to beat you to the painting, though," Mary noted.

"Yes, that caused me a slight bit of agony," Manchester admitted. "I contacted Messini as quickly as humanly possible, posing as a thief, and arranged to steal the Patrician Lady. When I arrived that night, masked and cloaked, he let me in the side door with a key he then put in his right coat pocket. I insisted that he leave a calling card on my behalf—a white feather from the skylight, to throw off Scotland Yard's suspicions concerning Mr. Messini's involvement."

"Why the white feather?" I demanded. "You have to know that is unwise."

He frowned at me.

"Unwise to use the calling card of a dead man?" He shook his head. "No, I thought it was the perfect distraction. At first, Messini was reluctant to leave the calling card for me, but then I reminded him of my promise to share with him a fourth of the lost Doge's treasure. He was all too eager after that."

"How did he get it up to the skylight?" Miss Jones wondered.

"It would be next to impossible to climb," Jack added.

"Now *that* was a trick," Manchester chuckled. "He wheeled a great platform ladder with stairs over to the skylight—it is normally used for hanging artwork high on the walls. He took off his coat, climbed up and hung the feather. While he did that," Manchester lifted a finger. "I reached in his pocket and took a wax mold of the key. Then I took the painting."

"You did not take it far, did you?" I lifted an eyebrow. Manchester shook his head.

"No, indeed! I hid it in my apartment, not a block away."

"Then you had another job to do," I went on. "You had to spread rumors, arouse public curiosity."

"That is why you spoke to *me* about a stolen painting," Miss Jones pointed out. Manchester shrugged.

"The news needed to reach the right ears. You see, I knew if I left a white feather," he gestured to me. "Inspector McDougal was bound to hear of it, come out of hiding, and investigate—which was just what I wanted. I knew he was the best."

I did nothing but wait for him to go on. Manchester cleared his throat.

"I had the key made, and then, before the gala, I distracted the guards by setting off a smoke screen in one of the wings, and returned the painting. Then I waited and watched. But, of course, I could *not* allow Mr. Messini to see me—for he could possibly identify me as both the thief and Mr. Manchester if he thought about it! That is why I ran from you." He glanced at Jack and Mary.

"What of the message on Messini's chair?" Mary asked. "Now that I consider it, the content makes perfect sense from your perspective—but how did you get it there?"

"Oh, yes, I left the message in the office right after I replaced the painting," he nodded. "I had only gambled on one thing: that some member of Scotland Yard, or even better—McDougal himself—would be there investigating. Luckily, you, Mr. Young and Miss Moore, were able to glimpse the message Mr. Messini received. I knew then that McDougal would hear of it and come tonight."

"You *knew* it," I said, then frowned. "Hm. Forgive me if I am less certain about your leap of logic."

Manchester looked at me squarely.

"Many of my father's friends are either policemen or detectives—and I have spent most of my adult life studying thieves and those who catch them. I knew by the manner of Mr. Young's questions that he and Miss Moore were investigating—besides the fact that *they* had cleverly managed *not* to get ushered out by Messini's guards." He gave Mary a look that bordered on affection. I took a step toward him, drawing his attention back.

"Tonight, you clearly got in the same way you did before—with a replicated key," I said. "What was your plan, then?"

"To stall for time," he said. "And try to get a rise out of Messini in hopes you would appear and hear his confession." He gestured to all of us. "And here you are."

"You knew he was armed," Miss Jones said.

"I also knew he was a terrible shot," Manchester smirked. "He never brought down any birds when he went hunting with my father."

"So now what is your plan?" I asked, sliding my gun back into its holster and folding my arms. "Have Messini murdered in prison?"

"Good heavens, no!" Manchester cried. "I wanted him ruined, certainly—not for my sake, but for my father's!" His face now bore genuine earnestness. "The more I learned of that man's treachery, the more disgusted I became that he would treat masterpieces of art like chattel, and betray his friends' trust for profit. But I do not wish him dead. Rather, if I have my way, he will be publicly exposed as the bottom-dweller he is, and someone more worthy will take over the Smith, and the sale of my Patrician Lady." He half smiled. "Though I will be sorry to see her go. She looked kindly down on our sitting room for as long as I can remember."

I felt Mary soften toward him, and even Miss Jones relaxed and put her gun away. Jack, however, remained stoic.

"That is all well and good," Jack said. "But I am afraid we still have a problem."

I glanced at him, knowing what he meant. But Miss Jones raised her eyebrows at him.

"What is that?"

Jack gestured to Manchester.

"He saw us yesterday as managers and employees of the Oxford Street Coffee House," Jack explained. "And today, he sees us as officers of Scotland Yard."

"Oh, you are worried about your cover!" Manchester sat up. "No need."

I canted my head and lifted an eyebrow.

"Really?"

"Truly," Manchester grinned. "After all, if I *did* tell anyone...I would have to confess that I learned your identities by stealing a painting from the Smith."

That was a good point, but I did not believe him. Not until the joviality faded from his face, and he met my eyes.

"I mean it, gentlemen," he said. "You have done me a great service tonight, and I admire your intellect and insight more than you imagine. I have been desperately hoping for years that somehow you, McDougal, might be able to help me in my endeavor. And you have." He nodded once. "I am indebted to you forever. I shan't breathe a word. I swear it on my father's grave."

"That is good enough for me," I declared, then held out my hand to him. "Good work, Mr. Manchester." I smiled. "Truth be told, we could use someone like you."

Manchester took my hand, but his eyes sparkled at Mary.

"I'll think about it." He drew himself up. "But for now, I would like to pay my respects to my Lady, and then go home and get a good night's rest."

"We'll walk with you," Mary offered brightly. He held out his arm and she took it. I sensed Jack frown at them, and Miss Jones watched Jack with a somber gaze. I kept my expression clear, turned, and opened the door for everyone. Together, the five of us trailed out through the domed gallery, and then down the hallway through which I had entered.

When at last we had stepped out into the chill, foggy alley once more, Mary glanced up at Manchester.

"Shall we be seeing you again, Edward?"

He beamed, clearly enjoying the fact that she had called him by his first name.

"I will be leaving town next week, but I should love to entertain all of you very soon at my townhouse for dinner, as soon as it is convenient!"

"We would be delighted," I inclined my head.

"Very good. Take my card, then," Manchester reached inside his coat and pulled out a card, and handed it to me. "I look forward to hearing from you!"

"Goodnight, sir," Miss Jones said. Manchester released Mary, faced us, and gave us a bow.

"Thank you all, once more, and God bless you."

I smiled, and bowed back, and then he waved, turned, and strode off down the alley into the shadows, whistling as he went. We all stood and listened to the tapping of his heels on the cobbles, and the whistled tune echoing through the mist. Then, the four of us stepped close together and headed back to the Oxford.

G

"THE TABLE DID NOT GET so full this case, did it?" Miss Jones commented as she raised her eyebrows at the table in the Crow's Nest. It was the next day, at two o'clock, and we had retreated with relief from our busy coffee house to our daily sanctuary. I chuckled, then eased down into my customary chair, careful to keep from spilling my cup of tea. Mary had made it perfectly: two lumps of sugar and an abundance of cream.

"That's because this one was resolved much quicker than usual," I commented, leaning back and taking a sip, then setting my cup down on the saucer with a clink. Miss Jones cast her always-serious gaze over the blueprints, the invitations, Manchester's note and the research on the Patrician Lady. She propped her right elbow on the tabletop, her hand holding a mug of her own favorite drink: black coffee with one lump of sugar. Soft mist rose from it, and filled the room with its earthy, rich scent—it almost banished the smell of dusty books, and the chemicals in the beakers behind me.

"Yes, this one was rather quick, didn't it?" Miss Jones mused. "I don't recall a case ever being opened and closed in a matter of two days."

"I suppose that's what happens when you have a brilliant man like Mr. Manchester doing most of the work for us," Mary commented, sweeping into the room, blue skirts rustling, her vanilla cappuccino held in both hands. I glanced up at her and could not keep from smiling—she answered it, and winked. Jack, who followed her like a brooding shadow, carried his own mug of completely unadulterated dark coffee carried in one hand.

"Brilliant. Ha," he scoffed, bright brown eyes flitting over the three of us. "I am yet to feel easy about the fact that he knows who we are."

"We could turn him in just as easily, Jack. You must see that," Miss Jones said, her voice taking on a softer tone she only used with him. He frowned in reply, but settled down onto his end of the couch beside Miss Jones, brushing the tails of his coat out of the way. Miss Jones cocked her head, trying to catch his eye, and gave him an uncharacteristic smile.

"You were brilliant as well," Miss Jones said. "Without your deduction that the painting would be too large to fit through the skylight, we would have been lost."

"Indeed, Jack," Mary added, coming to perch on her chair next to me and addressing him pointedly. "We would never have begun to suspect that it was an inside job."

Jack's head had come up at the sound of Mary's voice, and her words made him sit straighter and wipe the furrow from his brow. He smiled for the first time today, at her.

"Glad to be of service."

Miss Jones' eyes flickered, and she sat back. I addressed her.

"Tell me, Miss Jones—did you suspect Mr. Manchester from the beginning?"

She met my glance and gave me a wry look.

"To be honest, I did—and did not, at the same time."

Jack set his elbow on the armrest and regarded her.

"How so?"

She turned to him, frowned as she thought, then put her coffee down.

"I knew that he did not mean what he said about the missing painting," she said carefully. "But I also knew he was not wicked."

Jack glanced at me, flabbergasted.

"These women," he remarked, laughing. "Their art in reading us is positively occult—it unnerves me."

Miss Jones looked disturbed by this, until his eyes twinkled at her, and she grinned again.

"Frankly, I wouldn't have it any other way," I took a sip of my tea. "Where would we be, after all, Mr. Young, if we were set adrift without these ladies' penetrating insight?" I shot a warm look at Mary.

"I'll drink to that," Jack muttered good-naturedly, and lifted his cup.

"And we mustn't forget our lovely patrons," Mary added. "We might never have even heard anything was stolen in the first place!"

I laughed, and Miss Jones smirked.

"Speaking of patrons," Jack spoke up. "Did you hear Mr. Wilder telling me about a home brewer this morning?"

"No!" Miss Jones sat up. "Really? What kind? Do you know where he got it?"

"Oh, I was certain to ask him for details," Jack replied. "He said a friend of his was traveling in France and happened into a shop…"

I smiled to myself and allowed my shoulders to relax and my attention to wander as the topic of conversation amongst my colleagues turned to the roasting and serving of coffee. I watched their keen eyes and listened to their sharp wit, marveling at their intellect and how well they listened to each other. Once again, I was reminded of how proud I was that I had fought so hard against the old prejudices and persuaded Scotland Yard to install these two women as senior detectives at this post, citing the fact that there are many realms of society that a man cannot enter, but a woman can move with ease. And Jack—the young man was learning rapidly, there was no mistake. He was making a fine detective.

I smiled again, the sight of them warming me as surely as my tea did. They were brilliant, all of them, but they were still so fresh. Each case was exciting for them, each intrigue a cause for celebration. They had not seen what I had—they had not felt loss yet, or failure, or grief. Yes, they were brilliant. But they were not ready for real trials. Not yet.

The servant's bell above the door jangled. Mary stood up.

"That would be Lily with the sandwiches," she said.

"I'll help you," I said, set down my tea and followed her out of the room, leaving Jack and Miss Jones to their deep discussion of the merits of using an African coffee bean versus an Arabic bean.

Mary and I trotted down the stairs, then headed to the back door, through the storage room. Mary pulled the squeaking door open, letting afternoon sunlight spill through.

"Good day, Lily!" Mary greeted the woman outside. "How are you?"

"Hello, Mary," Lily, a very pretty red-headed young lady dressed in a white blouse, black skirt and frilly apron answered, pushing a long curl out of her face. Her pale cheeks were flushed, and her eyes were bright with exertion.

"I'm so sorry I'm late," Lily huffed, handing the lunch basket across the threshold to Mary. "I was just about to come to you when everything in my oven caught fire. I had to put the basket down almost in my doorway, run back and try to keep my entire confectionary from burning down."

"That's terrible!" I said, stepping closer. "Are you all right?"

Lily gave me a bright smile.

"Quite all right, sir," she said. "Just a little sooty—which is nothing new to me!"

"Will you come in? Sit down for a bit?" Mary invited. Lily was already shaking her head.

"I'm afraid I can't, but thank you. I have some raspberry tarts I need to finish." She lifted a slender hand and waved to us. "Enjoy! See you tomorrow in church!"

"Certainly! Goodbye, Lily!" Mary bid her, and shut the door as Lily departed.

"I'll carry that," I offered, and Mary handed me the basket. Together we left the back room and started toward the staircase.

"That's odd," Mary commented.

"What?"

"Lily burning something," she mused. "I've never heard of her burning anything before—she knows that stove better than the back of her hand."

"There is a first time for everything, I suppose," I answered as Mary attained the steps and began to climb. "Especially if one has too many projects to..." I slowed, then stopped, as I caught sight of an envelope sticking out from the lid of the basket. I hung the basket in the crook of my arm and pulled out the envelope.

I instantly went still.

No.

"Mac?" Mary's tone changed completely, and she stopped on the stairs. "Mac, what is it?"

I did not answer. Instead, with unsteady hands, I tore open the envelope, pulled out the single piece of paper, and read the black-inked, handwritten words three times before I took another breath.

> *Imitation is the sincerest form of flattery.*
> *Unless it is used against me.*
> *Mors solum initium est*

"Mac, what is it?"

My head came up. Mary stood in front of me, worried eyes fixed on my face. Ice filled my veins. I took a breath, then did not speak. I set the basket down on the coffee bar, swept past Mary and lunged up the stairs. I heard Mary's heels on the steps as she followed.

I shoved open the Crow's Nest's door and halted as Jack and Miss Jones' turned to regard me. Instantly, Miss Jones' gaze pierced me, and Jack's brow furrowed. I felt Mary come up beside me and take hold of my arm.

I held the letter in both hands, my head spinning. But there could be no mistake. Not this time. I met all their eyes, then managed to raise my voice enough to speak.

"Edward Manchester," I said. "Is in mortal danger."

Miss Jones leaped to her feet.

"What?" Jack cried. "What do you—"

"There is no time to explain," I held up my hand. "Mere seconds may mean the difference between his life and his death. We must get to him now, this moment."

Miss Jones met my gaze.

"Then let's go."

I nodded, turned and raced back down the stairs. Mary hurried after, then Miss Jones, then Jack.

"What about the customers?" Jack called over the racket of our shoes against the steps.

"We have to close for the afternoon," I said as I hopped off the last stair and strode to the back room. "A death in the family. Miss Jones?"

"No, all of my relatives are already dead, remember?" she said as we crowded in past the bags of beans.

"Jack?" I called.

"What?" he yelped. "Oh, please not me—if I pretend to kill off my last aunt, I'll have nowhere to go for Christmas!"

"I have an aunt that hasn't spoken to me for a year," Mary said, pulling on her jacket. "And she lives in Derbyshire. She'll do."

I smiled at her and donned my hat.

"Very well," I said. "We are all going to Mary's aunt's funeral. Shall we?"

We whooshed out of the back room, all wearing our coats and hats, performed a double-door exit through the front of the Oxford, and I locked the house behind us. Then, the bright sun beaming down on us, I held out my arm to Mary, and she took it. Jack did the same for Miss Jones, and together we hurried as fast as we could down the walk that followed the bustle of Oxford Street.

Don't miss out!

Visit the website below and you can sign up to receive emails whenever Alydia Rackham publishes a new book. There's no charge and no obligation.

https://books2read.com/r/B-A-MQLEB-VHWBD

BOOKS 2 READ

Connecting independent readers to independent writers.

Did you love *The Oxford Street Coffee House Detectives and the Case of the Young Patrician Lady*? Then you should read *The Ignominious Mister Tipp*[1] by Alydia Rackham!

[2]

An unlikely duo and an ice-cold murder case... Lucinda Holliday--an educated lady with fiery red hair and an aloof disposition--must bargain help from the striking-but-volatile American, Mr. Tipp: a disgraced detective turned opium addict...For he is the only man on earth who can possibly solve the mystery of her father's senseless murder.*Plunge into the romance and danger of 1870's London as this incompatible pair tangle with the cold case that destroyed both their lives, all while being haunted and hunted by the most elusive and insidious murderer in the world.*

Read more at https://alydiarackham642036291.wordpress.com/.

---

1. https://books2read.com/u/4jY9qD

2. https://books2read.com/u/4jY9qD

Also by Alydia Rackham

Alydia Rackham's Retellings
Bauldr's Tears: Retelling Loki's Fate
Ghost: Retelling the Phantom of the Opera
The Tailor of Semenov: Retelling the Legend of Anastasia

Lady Rackham
Lady Rackham: An Unusual Tale of Piracy Upon the High Seas
Blackbeard's Sword: The Continuing Adventures of Captain Lady
Rackham

Stardust
Stardust

The Curse-Breaker Series
Scales: A Fresh Telling of Beauty and the Beast
Glass: Retelling the Snow Queen
Tide: Retelling the Little Mermaid
Curse-Maker: The Tale of Gwiddon Crow

The Legacy of Constantin
The Last Constantin: A Novel of the Original Vampire

The Pendywick Place
The Mute of Pendywick Place and the Torn Page
The Mute of Pendywick Place and the Scarlet Gown
The Mute of Pendywick Place and the River Thames
The Mute of Pendywick Place and the Irish Gamble
The Mute of Pendywick Place and the Ghost of Robin Hood's Bay
The Mute of Anthony College and the Three Professors
Dear David: Being the Private Diary of Basil Atticus Collingwood
The Ignominious Mister Tipp

The Tailor of Semenov
The Tailor of Semenov - Part 1
The Tailor of Semenov - Part Two
The Tailor of Semenov - Part 3
The Tailor of Semenov - Part 4

Standalone
The Last Scene
Knight of Novus: A Post-Dystopia Novel
Amatus
Linnet and the Prince
The Oxford Street Coffee House Detectives and the Case of the Young
Patrician Lady

The Web of Tenebrae: The Chronicle of KL-62

Watch for more at https://alydiarackham642036291.wordpress.com/.

About the Author

Alydia Rackham is a daughter of Jesus Christ. She has written more than thirty original novels of many genres, including fantasy, time-travel, steampunk, modern romance, historical fiction, science fiction, and allegory. She is also a singer, actress, avid traveler, artist, and animal lover. Read more at https://alydiarackham642036291.wordpress.com/.